RAMBUNCTIOUS
RATTLER

THE WILDS is pleased to present this
book as part of our mission to
provide resources that will help people
grow spiritually. Please note that
THE WILDS may not completely endorse
the contents of this book. Each book we
offer is carefully considered by our staff
and chosen because of its overall
message or impact. We encourage every
reader to read with discernment
and to compare everything to
the Scriptures, the only book we
can depend on to be without error.

Bob Jones University Press
Greenville, South Carolina 29614

Library of Congress Cataloging-in-Publication Data

Fremont, Walter G., 1924-

    Rambunctious Rattler / Walter G. Fremont and Susan W. Young.

    p. cm.

    SUMMARY: After twelve-year-old Gil buys a horse with a history, he finds that God has many lessons for him to learn.

    ISBN 1-57924-262-6 (pbk)

    I. Young, Susan W., 1956 II. Title.

    PZ7.F8868 Ram 1999

    [Fic]--ddc21

                            99-23179

                               CIP

Rambunctious Rattler

Edited by Elizabeth B. Berg

Designed by Douglas R. Young

Cover and illustrations by Kathy Pflug

© 1999 by Bob Jones University Press

Greenville, South Carolina 29614

ISBN 1-57924-262-6

15 14 13 12 11 10 9 8 7 6 5 4 3 2 1

Contents

Chapter 1

Gil smiled. He had a plan. He was going to buy a horse. Now he had to convince Dad that his plan would work. That would be the hard part. He could hear Dad now. "Son, a horse is a big responsibility. It's not like other pets. You can't just bury him in the back yard when something happens to him. You need to have a plan." Dad would want all the facts, so Gil had plenty to give him.

Dad's car turned into the driveway and pulled up to the garage door. There's no time like the present, Gil could hear his grandfather say. Gil jumped off the porch and ran to the car. He skidded to a stop as the car door swung open. "Dad, you got a minute?"

"Sure, Son, what's on your mind?" Dad handed Gil his briefcase. "Must be pretty important. You didn't even let me get in the house first."

"It's not just important; it's super important!" Gil matched his stride to his dad's. "You see, there's something I want real bad, and I've got a plan to get it. You always tell me to set a goal and then plan how to reach it. So that's what I've done."

"Well, let me kiss your mother and see how long it is 'til supper, then we'll sit down and you can tell me all about it." Dad tousled Gil's hair. "Can you wait another minute or two?"

"Sure, Dad, no problem." He grinned. "I'll be in the den."

It seemed like forever before Dad came into the den. How long does it take for one little welcome-home kiss and a question about supper anyway? Gil sighed. It seemed like he always had to wait for something or someone. Life was never simple.

"Supper's in twenty minutes. You think you can fill me in on this plan of yours in twenty minutes?" Dad pushed himself back in his recliner. "Okay, Buddy, shoot. What is it that you want 'real bad'?"

"You know how I'm always begging to go ride horses, but you tell me the stables charge too much to make it worth it? Well, I think I've solved the problem." Gil cleared his throat. "I'm going to buy my own horse so I can ride him any time I want to. I talked to Granddad, and he says I can keep the horse up at his place, and I asked Mom what she thought about the idea, and she didn't say no, so I thought I'd see what you think. I'll pay for him myself . . ."

"Hold on there, Buddy. Do you have any idea how much a good horse costs? You're talking about a lot of money here."

"I know, Dad; that's why I came up with a plan. Don't you want to hear my plan?"

"Sure, I'll listen to your plan. But let me warn you, you're going to have a hard time finding a horse you can afford."

"But that's just it, Dad, I already have. That's the beauty of it. I already know where there's a registered quarter horse I can get for only $400."

"$400? A registered quarter horse?"

"Yes, sir. I told Pastor Mike that I was looking for a horse to buy, and he called his dad. His dad has a horse farm in Texas, you know."

"You're planning to go all the way to Texas to get this horse?"

"No, Dad. Pastor Mike's dad has a friend who has a horse farm in Georgia. He has a three-year-old registered quarter horse that he wants to sell for $400. He said he'd even throw in a saddle, a bridle, and a halter for an extra hundred bucks. I can get a horse and everything to go with it for $500."

"Now hold on, Son. Nobody sells a perfectly good registered quarter horse for $400. They go for at least $1,500. There must be something wrong with the horse."

"All I know, Dad, is that Pastor Mike thinks it's a good deal. And he said he'd be glad to drive me down to Georgia to see it. He even has a horse trailer we can use to bring the horse back."

"Sounds to me like you've already made up your mind." Dad put his hands behind his head. "And how are you planning to pay for a registered quarter horse?"

"I have it all worked out. I have about $200 saved up from my paper route, and Granddad said he'd loan me the rest. He said I could work for him every Saturday morning, and he'll pay me $10 a week. After school and in the summer, I can mow yards and do odd jobs for the neighbors. Then around Christmastime I can sell mistletoe again. I can do it, Dad; I know I can."

"There's more to a horse than just buying him. How're you going to feed him?"

"Granddad says his pasture's big enough for two horses, and Pastor Mike says I can buy hay and sweet feed from him in the winter time. With that and vet bills he figured I should plan on about $300 a year to take care of him."

"And you're sure Granddad said he didn't mind your keeping the horse at his place?"

"He said he'd be glad to have him. Granddad can see the pasture from the big window at the side of the house, and having a horse in the pasture will give him something else to watch besides the squirrels and the birds. He said I could use his shed to store the hay and sweet feed, and the horse could stay in there during the winter."

"Son, I'm proud of you. For twelve and a half, you're showing real maturity. Looks like you've thought of everything. Your plan just might work if this horse really is only $400 and isn't on his last legs. I'll talk it over with your mother and give you an answer in a couple of days."

"A couple of days!" Gil fell backwards on the couch.

"You've waited this long, Gil. A few more days won't hurt. Besides, I want to check out this horse and make sure this is a good deal."

"And if it all checks out, will you say yes?"

"I always ask God for wisdom when I'm making a major decision. This falls into that category because it will involve a lot of work, responsibility, and commitment on your part. I want you to do the right thing with your time and money. If it is His will, then He will provide all you need to take care of this horse."

"But what if the horse is sold by the time you check?"

"If that horse is supposed to be yours, it will be there when you get ready to buy it. Sometimes God uses circumstances to show us exactly what His will is. Remember, God is in complete control, so you just have to trust Him. Now, I think supper is about ready. I don't know about you, but that fried chicken sure smells good, and all this talk about hard work has made me hungry."

As Dad prayed before they ate, Gil prayed silently. "God, a couple of days is a long time, and you know how much I want this horse. Help me trust you to take care of everything 'cause it sure is hard to wait."

Two days later, Gil ran down the stairs to breakfast, buttoning his shirt as he jumped three steps at a time. He smelled the bacon and eggs cooking on the stove, and he could hear Dad and Mom talking.

"Okay, Dad, what is it? Yes or no?" Gil stuffed his shirt into his pants as he came around the corner. "I can't wait another millisecond."

"Hold your horses, Son. We'll talk about it over breakfast."

"But, Dad, that's exactly what I want to do—'hold my horse'—but I don't have one yet." Gil slid into his chair. Things didn't sound good. Usually when Dad said "let's talk about it," it meant no. He didn't know how Dad expected him to eat breakfast. The suspense was killing him.

Finally, Dad pushed back his plate. "I got the telephone number from Pastor Mike and called the owner of the horse." Dad took a swallow of coffee. "He told me he breeds and trains show horses. I told him I didn't understand how he could let one go for only $400. He said he knew that did seem awful cheap but that there was a good reason for it. He can't use this horse as a show horse because he has a slight limp. He's also a spooker."

"What's a spooker?" Gil pulled his legs up under the chair and leaned forward.

"That's a horse that is afraid of just about everything. This particular horse must have had a pretty bad scare at one point, so now he jumps at anything that is unfamiliar to him. If he hears a rustling in the woods, he rears straight up."

"So no one can even ride him?" Gil was having a hard time swallowing his breakfast.

"Actually, the owner said he's a good riding horse when he's not scared. He also said that it is possible to train a horse not to spook at every sound. It takes some work, but it can be done."

"Did he say what scared the horse the first time?"

"He said he'd tell us the story when we came down to see him. And since you have a day off from school on Friday and I'm caught up at the office, I figured it might be a good day to do just that."

Gil almost fell out of his chair. "Friday? Is this a yes? I get to buy him?"

"It means we'll go down and look him over. You know what Granddad always says: 'Never buy a pig in a poke or a horse in a barn.'"

Gil laughed. "Well, I'm not planning to buy any pigs, but I'll make sure I take the horse out of the barn and ride him before I buy him."

Chapter 2

Friday was a perfect day for a drive to Georgia. Mom had packed a big lunch so they wouldn't have to stop to eat along the way. Gil was glad Mom always planned ahead. He didn't want to stop for anything before he got to see the horse.

"Well, I think we're ready to go." Pastor Mike checked the trailer hitch one last time. "Sure hope for your sake, Gil, this trailer doesn't come back empty."

"Me too." Gil slid to the middle of the truck seat and straddled the gearshift. "I don't care if this horse is blind in both eyes and lame; I'm buying him."

"Whoa there, Gil." Dad slid in beside him. "I thought we'd agreed that you'd check this horse out before you decided to buy him."

"I know, Dad, but I'm just afraid I won't get another chance like this one. It's like you said, it isn't often you can find a horse for $400."

"But blind and lame? I'm not sure that kind of horse would be much good." Dad hooked his seat belt and rolled down the window. "What do you think, Mike?"

Pastor Mike slammed the door and leaned forward to turn the key in the ignition. "Well, I have to admit, blind and lame doesn't make for much of a horse. You might as well buy a fence post and ride it." The engine roared to life.

"You know what I mean." Gil moved his knee out of the way so Pastor Mike could shift gears. "I wouldn't really buy him if he were blind and lame. But I don't know what I'll do if I can't buy him."

"Son, you always have to be ready for a little disappointment. Not everything turns out the way we want it to. Just remember that the Lord has a plan for your life. If this horse isn't part of His plan, you wouldn't want it anyway. And if this isn't the one, there'll be another one."

Gil stared straight ahead. He knew Dad was right. He shouldn't get his heart set on something he hadn't even seen.

"Just leave it up to the Lord, Gil. You need to be less fearful about things and just trust Him." Dad put his arm across the back of the seat. "It's a hard lesson to learn, but it's well worth learning."

The highway to Georgia was lined with dogwood trees bursting with new leaves and blossoms. The fresh spring air blowing in the windows of the truck carried the scent of blooming flowers.

"Isn't it wonderful how God shares so much beauty with us?" Dad pointed out one tree covered with pink blossoms. Dad began to sing "How Great Thou Art," and Gil and Pastor Mike joined in.

They sang one song after another until they could sing no more. Gil closed his eyes. He tried to imagine what the horse looked like. Black maybe? No, probably brown. Maybe with white socks or a white star in the middle of his forehead. It didn't matter. He just wanted to get there and see him.

"Gil," Dad's voice broke into his thoughts. "Gil, we're almost there."

Gil's eyes flew open. He must have fallen asleep.

"From the looks of the sign back there, we have about seventy-five miles to go," Dad pointed behind him. "We'd better break out those sandwiches your mother packed. I hate to do business on an empty stomach."

Gil didn't think he'd be able to eat, but he managed to gulp down two huge ham sandwiches, an apple, potato chips, and a brownie. No one could complain about being hungry when Mom was in charge of food.

Pastor Mike reached across him to point. "There's the sign."

They turned off the main road onto a dirt driveway lined on both sides with a white board fence. Green pasture stretched as far as Gil could see, unbroken except for an occasional tree. Gil hadn't expected the place to be so big. Maybe this meant the horse was a good one. They stopped in front of a large white barn.

"We're here." Pastor Mike put the truck in gear and set the brake.

Gil nudged Dad. "Hurry up, Dad. Let's get out."

"Can't get out 'til my seat belt's unbuckled. Besides, the horse isn't going anywhere." Dad laughed and pushed open the door.

Gil jumped out after his dad. Pastor Mike was talking to a man wearing cowboy boots and a cowboy hat.

"This is Gil," Pastor Mike said. "Gil, this is Al Burgess, the owner of this place."

"Nice to meet you, sir." Gil gave the man's hand a quick shake. "Where's the horse?"

Dad came up behind him. "Don't be in such a hurry, Son."

"It's all right. I was the same way when I was a boy." The man stuck out his hand. "Al Burgess. I believe we talked on the phone."

"Walt Freeman." He took the offered hand. "I appreciate your giving me more information over the phone. I just wanted to make sure we weren't coming all this way for nothing."

"That's understandable. People try to pass off all kinds of things these days." Al turned to Gil. "You ready to see the horse?"

"Yes, sir." Gil fell in step with the man. "Does he have a name?"

"His name's Rattler." The man lifted his fingers to his lips and let out a long, loud whistle. Over the rise of the hill, a magnificent reddish brown horse appeared. "Here he comes."

Gil couldn't believe his eyes. The horse's powerful legs pounded the grass, the muscles of his chest working as he ran. The horse ran right up to the fence and stopped.

Al gave Gil a carrot. "You might as well meet and make friends."

Gil held the carrot out. The horse nuzzled it and took it. Gil touched the soft nose.

"Looks like he likes you. He's usually afraid of strangers."

"I think we're going to be great friends. Don't you, Dad?"

"It does look that way, Gil. But we've got some questions to get answered before you get too attached. Remember?"

"Sure, Dad, I remember. 'Don't buy a pig in a poke.' Isn't that what you mean? But Rattler's not in a poke. I can see him plain as day. And he looks good to me. I didn't even see a limp when he came running over. Are you sure he has one, Mr. Burgess?"

"Call me Al. And yes, he surely does have a limp. Probably not so you'd notice. Just bad enough to keep him out of competition. He would have been a great show horse if he hadn't been bitten by that snake."

"A snake?"

"Yep, a big old ugly rattlesnake. That's what turned him into a spooker."

The horse nuzzled Gil's shoulder. "I think he wants another carrot," Gil said.

"What he's looking for is sugar. He knows I usually have some cubes with me, and he's wanting to know if you have some too." Al reached into his shirt pocket. "Here, give him these. Hold your hand out flat. He'll pick them up."

The horse took the sugar cubes from Gil's hand and then backed away from the fence.

"Looks like he's afraid I might want them back."

"That very well may be. Rattler's afraid of just about everything."

"And that's why he's a spooker?"

"That's right, kid. Any horse that is as afraid of things as Rattler is definitely a spooker."

"So he wasn't afraid of things until after the snake bit him?"

"Well now, there's the story. Fear can be a powerful thing. It can change a man or a horse. How about we go inside and get a glass of iced tea, and I'll tell you Rattler's story from the very beginning?"

Chapter 3

Al led the way to the house. Once inside the large farm kitchen, he motioned for the others to sit at the table. He brought a pitcher of iced tea and four glasses to the table.

"Boy, Mom sure would love this kitchen, wouldn't she, Dad?" Gil took a long swallow of tea. "She could cook up a storm."

"Yes, my wife loved this kitchen. I'm afraid since she's been gone, it hasn't gotten much use, though." Al pulled out a chair, turned it around, and sat in it backwards. "She's been gone almost two years now. Died of bone cancer. Happened real fast." He rubbed his hand along the chair back. "Now it's just me and my boy, Tim."

"We're sorry to hear that, Mr. Burgess," said Pastor Mike.

"Thank you. The Lord has seen us through. I don't know what we'd have done without Him." Al lifted his head. "But I didn't bring you in here to tell you my life story. I brought you in here to tell you Rattler's story. And by the way, the name's Al. When you call me Mr. Burgess, I feel like you're talking to my father. So please just call me Al." He grinned and slapped Pastor Mike on the shoulder. "Now where was I?"

"You were getting ready to tell us about Rattler." Gil emptied his glass.

"Right you are. Here, let me fill that up for you again." Al filled Gil's glass and set the pitcher in the middle of the table. "Now while I'm telling, you just keep drinking your tea, and if you run out, just fill 'er up yourself. I can't tell a story and do anything else at the same time." Al took a long drink and set his glass on the table.

"When Rattler was born, we named him Red Adair—Red because of his coloring and Adair after his sire, a prize-winning quarter horse himself. He was a fine colt, and we were sure he would be a prize winner like his father. But unfortunately, he wasn't as well behaved as his father. He was rambunctious and had a streak of mischief in him."

"What kind of mischief?" Gil leaned forward.

"Getting out of the fence mischief. He figured out how to lift the latch on the gate and escape from the pasture. More than once we found him on the outside of the gate just waiting for us to let him back in. Funny, he could let himself out, but he never could figure out how to get back in. Or maybe he just waited 'til we found him so he could enjoy the joke."

"Wow, a horse with a sense of humor. Granddad will like that." Gil grinned at his dad.

"I guess that's what he has all right, a sense of humor. But one day it didn't turn out to be so funny. He let himself out of the gate and decided to go exploring. I don't know where he'd been, but when I found him he was lying in the lane that leads to the house. At first I thought he'd broken his leg, but then I saw that his back left leg was swollen. When I looked at it, I found two definite fang marks. I immediately got on my truck radio and called Tim to bring the front loader. It was the only way we could get him back to the barn."

"Once we got him to the barn, I made a poultice of flaxseed and wrapped it over the bite. It's the best thing for drawing out the poison. I knew it would be about three days before the swelling would go down. All we could do was pray that he would recover. It was a hard time, hardest on Tim. Rattler was the first horse he had ever owned."

"Did you ever find the snake that bit him?" asked Dad.

"We sure did. Tim decided that since all we could do was wait, we might as well go hunting for that snake. We didn't want him to get into the pasture and bite another one of the horses. We followed Rattler's tracks and searched the wooded area near where we had found him. Not far away we found the snake near a log, dead."

"Dead? But who killed him?" Gil was on the edge of his seat.

"Apparently, Rattler had killed him. He must have stepped on him several times in his fright."

"Wow, he *is* a great horse."

"Do you know, that snake was one of the biggest we'd ever seen. We carried him back to the barn and skinned him. He was six feet two inches long and had ten buttons on his tail. Some people say the buttons on a rattler's tail tell his age; if so, this guy had been around a long time. We were glad to get rid of him. We stretched his skin on the wall over Rattler's stall. People heard about it and came from town to see it. They could hardly believe it. Everyone was surprised that Rattler survived the bite. We told them it was good old-fashioned flaxseed poultices and the grace of God that pulled him through."

"And that's how he got his limp and his name, right?"

"Sure is. Everyone took to calling him the rattlesnake horse, so we changed his name to Rattler. Once he was up and around, we discovered he had a slight limp, not enough to slow him up, but just enough to keep him out of show competition. Nearly broke Tim's heart. He'd been looking forward to showing his very own horse, but it was not going to happen. He'd hoped there'd be no lasting effects from the bite, but he was disappointed. We decided it wasn't in God's plan for Rattler to be a show horse. Tim'll have other opportunities. He knows that, and I do too. All this just taught us to trust the Lord and not get our sights set on things down here. God's in control, so we just wait and trust. That's what I always tell Tim."

"But there's something I don't understand. If Tim loves this horse so much, why is he selling him?"

" 'Cause I need the money." The screen door banged. A dark-haired boy stood in the doorway to the kitchen. His head almost touched the top of the door frame.

"Come on in, Tim." Al pulled out a chair. "Fellows, this is my son and right-hand man, Tim. Tim, this is Gil, his dad, and his youth pastor, Mike. They're the ones interested in Rattler."

Tim sat across from Gil. "He's a good horse. If I didn't need the money, I'd keep him."

"Boy, I don't see how you can give him up. He's great."

"We just don't have a place to keep a horse that can't earn his keep. Dad and I are running things tight as it is. Another horse to feed just won't help. Besides, the $400 will sure help toward my college tuition in another year."

"Well, if my dad says I can buy him, I promise I'll take good care of him."

"We might as well go take another look at him." Dad stood up. "A horse with a story like that must have good strong qualities. Are you sure you can't get more than $400 for him?"

"Dad," Gil pulled at his sleeve.

"Oh, we could get a lot more for him, sir." Tim stepped away from the table. "If we didn't tell anyone his shortcomings. Most people don't even notice his limp."

"I sure didn't," Gil said.

"And no one would know he's a spooker until they tried to ride him. And we wouldn't have to tell anyone about his bad habit of opening the gate latch, either. We could probably get triple the price if we kept all that to ourselves. But that just wouldn't be honest. Dad's always taught me that honesty is not only the best policy but the right policy. And he's always backed it up with

Romans 12:17: 'Provide things honest in the sight of all men.' So you see, we had to tell you those things; and in light of all that, $400 is a fair price."

Al held open the screen door. "We've been praying that the right person would come along, someone who would love Rattler as much as we have. We do want him to have a good home."

"Sounds like Gil's been praying for a horse, and you've been praying for a home for Rattler, and the Lord has answered both prayers at one time." Dad swung his arm around Gil's shoulders. "Gil, my boy, you need to go give that horse a test ride. It looks like you're going to get yourself a horse."

"I wish I could ride him home." Gil stopped and stared out at the horse.

Pastor Mike laughed. "It's two hundred miles back to Greendale, Gil. I think the horse trailer is a better idea. Let's see if Rattler thinks so too."

Chapter 4

Gil put Rattler through his paces in the upper pasture. First a slow walk, then a trot, a canter, and then a gallop. The wind rushed around him as he leaned down toward Rattler's neck. "That's a boy. Show me what you can do."

After a few turns around the pasture, he walked Rattler back to the fence.

"Well, Son, what do you think?" Dad held the reins as Gil slid to the ground. "Is he everything you thought he'd be?"

"And more!" Gil rubbed Rattler's soft nose. "He rides great. You can't even tell he's got a limp."

"Well, I'm satisfied if you are." Dad traced the diamond of white on Rattler's forehead. "I think you've got yourself a horse."

Gil reached in his back pocket and pulled out his billfold. It bulged with crisp new twenty-dollar bills, which he and Dad had withdrawn from the bank, and the $300 Granddad had loaned him. "$500, which includes the saddle and bridle, right?"

"That's right, Gil, plus the halter." Al unlocked the pasture gate. "Just give the money to Tim. It's his, anyway."

Gil walked slowly toward him, counting as he went. ". . . 420, 440, 460, 480, 500. Here you go." He handed the money to Tim.

"Thanks." Tim stuffed the folded bills into his jeans. "By the way, I have some things you'll need to take care of Rattler." He led the way into the barn. "I'll throw them in as part of the deal." Tim handed Gil two lead ropes, a bucket, a curry comb, a brush, a mane and tail comb, and a hoof pick.

Gil smiled. "Thanks, that's mighty generous of you."

"My dad always says, 'Make sure the customer is happy with the deal.'" Tim and Gil stepped back out into the sunshine.

Al had Rattler waiting by the trailer. Gil put the bucket of things in the bed of the truck beside the bridle and saddle.

"May I try getting him into the trailer?" Gil held his hand out toward the rope.

"You sure you want to?" Al asked.

"I might as well get used to doing all the work. I'll have to when we get home."

Gil took the lead rope from Al. He talked softly to Rattler.

"Just take it slow." Pastor Mike spoke up from beside the trailer. "You don't want to scare him."

Gil moved very slowly toward the trailer, letting the rope remain slack. "Come on Rattler; there's nothing to be afraid of." Gil stepped clear as Rattler reached the edge of the trailer. "That's right, boy, just go on in."

But Rattler had a mind of his own. He began to buck and rear. He turned his head from side to side, flaring his nostrils and snorting all the while. The rope jerked in Gil's hand.

"Watch out, Gil!" Dad yelled. "Don't let him land on you."

With one last kick of his heels, Rattler stood still.

"I may just have to push him in." Gil wiped the dirt and sweat from his face.

Tim laughed. "No, what you need to do is persuade him that this really is a good idea."

"How do I do that?"

"Watch and learn the secrets of horse persuasion." Tim disappeared into the barn.

"What's he gone to get?" Gil asked.

"Just something that will convince Rattler that getting into that trailer isn't such a bad idea," Al said.

Tim returned with a bucket and handed it to Gil.

"What's this?" Gil peered into the bucket.

"Sweet feed."

"Sweet feed? What's in it?"

"Corn, bran, and oats mixed with molasses. Horses love it."

"What am I supposed to do with it?"

"Nothing yet." Tim disappeared into the barn again. This time he returned with an armload of alfalfa hay. "I'll put this hay in the front end of the trailer. Then you give Rattler a taste of the sweet feed, and he'll follow you right in. Works every time."

Sure enough, when Rattler got a taste of the sweet feed, he followed Gil right up to the trailer. The scent of fresh hay took him the rest of the way in.

"That's a good lesson to learn, Gil. Give an animal food he likes, and you can get him to do almost anything." Pastor Mike closed and latched the end gate of the trailer.

"Yes, and growing boys are just about the same way." Dad slapped Gil on the shoulder. "Feed them well, and you've got them right where you want them. And speaking of feeding them well, I think we'd better hit the road so we can be home in time for a late supper."

"You'll have to drive slower with the trailer weighted down like that." Al checked the locks on the trailer. "Why don't you just stay and eat with us? We eat early around here to give us the last few hours of daylight to bed down the horses. It'll be no trouble to throw a couple more steaks on the grill."

Gil looked from Al to his dad and back again. There's nothing he liked better than a steak fresh off the grill, unless of course it was Mom's fried chicken. He could hear his stomach growling.

"Please, Dad?"

Dad looked at Gil. "Your mother's not looking for us until after dark. We accept. Is that all right with you, Mike?"

"Sounds great to me. My calendar's free all evening."

"Tim," Al turned to his son. "You and Gil get Rattler out of the trailer and let him back into the pasture. No sense his staying all locked up until it's absolutely necessary."

They ate supper on the patio. The steaks were tender and juicy and seasoned just right. There were potatoes baked in the coals, corn on the cob, fresh tomatoes, and to top it off, homemade vanilla ice cream. What a feast!

Gil leaned back in his chair and rubbed his stomach.

Al laughed. "Did you get enough to eat, Gil?"

"Sure did. I don't think I'll be able to eat again for a week."

"I doubt that," said his dad. "You'll be hungry again by the time we get home." Dad pushed back his chair. "Now, let's help Tim and Al clean up, and then we'll hit the road."

"You don't need to help with the cleanup." Al stood up from the table. "Tim and I have it down to a science. We're quite a team. Besides, you need to get going so your wife doesn't worry."

Tim and Gil got Rattler settled in the trailer again.

"It seems a shame he has to ride back here all by himself. Oh well, at least we'll be going the same direction," said Gil.

Pastor Mike led in a word of prayer for God's protection on the road. Gil and his dad said goodbye to their new friends.

"Come see us again sometime." Al shook Gil's hand. "And you just call us if you need any advice. No one knows Rattler like we do. Treat him well, and he'll be a good horse for you. Be firm but gentle, and you'll have a friend for life."

Chapter 5

Gil was having trouble sitting still as Pastor Mike maneuvered the truck and trailer onto the highway. The extra weight in the back made driving more difficult.

"A thousand pounds of horse flesh sure makes a difference," Pastor Mike said as he pulled out onto the highway. "You might as well get comfortable, Gil. We won't be moving quite as fast going this way."

Nobody said much as the miles passed. Gil scrunched down, leaned his head against the back of the seat, and closed his eyes.

"Hey! Look out!"

Gil jerked up. "What happened?"

"That big white car up ahead just came out of nowhere and passed me on the wrong side. I'm surprised there was enough of a shoulder for him to even drive on. He was doing at least ninety, maybe even a hundred. He'd better be careful," Pastor Mike said.

"It looks like he's weaving back and forth." Gil pointed at the car up ahead. "I'll bet he's been drinking."

Grazing a cement bridge abutment, the white car careened off the road.

"He just missed that bridge!" Dad shouted. "He's going to flip over!"

The car did not flip but jumped a small stream and came to rest in an open field.

"We'd better see if we can help. Someone's got to be hurt." Pastor Mike eased the truck and trailer off the road and stopped.

"Gil, you'd better check on Rattler. Your dad and I will go see if there's anything we can do."

Gil ran to the back of the truck. Peering in the small openings at the side of the trailer, he spoke softly to Rattler. "It's okay, boy. We're just stopping to see if we can help. Nothing's going to hurt you. It's all right." The restless stamping of the horse's hooves stilled. Rattler whinnied and snorted. "I know you don't like the trailer. But we'll be home soon and then I'll get you out. Just hold on while we check out this crazy driver. I'll be right back." He ran to the white car.

"Anybody hurt?"

"Looks like the driver's hurt pretty bad. I can't tell for sure. I can't get the door open. It's stuck in the dirt." Pastor Mike tried again to open the door on the driver's side. "I can't tell if there's anyone else in the car."

"Let me give you a hand, Mike." Gil's dad motioned for Gil to join them. "Come on, Gil; help us get this door open."

The three of them finally managed to pull open the driver's door. The unconscious driver was leaning forward on the steering wheel. Blood flowed steadily from a cut on his head. Pastor Mike felt for a pulse.

"It's faint, but it's there. We'd better not move him, though. He could have injured his neck or back. We'll wait for the ambulance." Pastor Mike pulled a clean handkerchief from his pocket and pressed it against the cut to stop the blood.

A few minutes later a passing state patrol car stopped and radioed for an ambulance. Later, as the driver was loaded into the ambulance, one of the state patrolmen spoke to Mike, Gil, and his dad.

"I'm Officer Madison." The officer held up an empty whiskey bottle. "Looks like we found the culprit. After drinking all this, I'm surprised he could stay on the road at all. Did you fellas see what happened?"

Pastor Mike and Dad filled the officer in on what had occurred from the moment the white car had passed them.

The officer turned the bottle slowly in his hands as they talked. "You're pretty lucky, you know. He could've run into you before he ran off the road. He was probably too drunk to know he was even in a car."

"Well, sir, we don't consider it luck," Pastor Mike said. "Before we left Georgia, we asked God to protect us as we drove back to Greendale. It was His mighty hand of protection that kept us safe."

The officer looked from one to the other. "You know, this isn't the first time I've had someone tell me that it was God who had protected them. Personally, I have a hard time believing that God has time to look out for everyone. And I sure don't think He'd waste His time looking out for me."

"God doesn't consider it a waste of time to take care of His children. God protects His children because He loves them."

"Isn't everybody one of God's children?"

"Only those who have accepted His Son Jesus Christ as their personal Savior."

Gil prayed that God would use what Pastor Mike was saying to help the officer understand that he needed to be saved. He knew Dad was praying too.

"I've heard that before. A friend of mine keeps telling me that I need to get saved. At least I think that's the word he uses. I've never paid much attention to all that, though. I've never been quite sure what I needed to be saved from."

"The Bible says we have all sinned and that the punishment for sin is death. God sent Jesus to die on the cross so we can be saved from that punishment. Jesus paid the price for all our sins."

"Well, I'm a church member. Doesn't that count for anything?"

"Not when it comes to being saved from eternal punishment in hell. God tells us in the Bible that 'The wages of sin is death; but the gift of God is eternal life through Jesus Christ our Lord.' We can be saved only by accepting Him as our Savior." Pastor Mike pulled a New Testament from his pocket and carefully explained I John 5:11-13, John 1:12, and Romans 10:9-13. "Would you like to accept Him right now?"

"Now? Right here?"

"Sure. You can pray and ask God to save you from your sin right now. Then you will know that He is with you, protecting you and helping you every day."

"Right now, right here?"

Gil kept praying as Pastor Mike showed the officer how to tell God he was a sinner and ask Jesus Christ to save him. Just as they finished, his partner came up.

"I think we've about wrapped things up." The big man held out his hand to Pastor Mike. "I'm Officer Radburn. You sure are lucky that guy didn't just run over you."

"That's what Officer Madison was just telling us. But like we told him, it wasn't luck; it was God's hand that kept us safe."

"You guys must be Christians. They're the only ones I know who talk like that."

"Yes, we're Christians. What about you? Are you a Christian?"

"Well, I went forward in a revival meeting several years ago and asked God to save me. But I haven't been to church in almost three years." Officer Radburn took off his hat and wiped his forehead. "Things like this make me think that maybe I should get back to it. You just don't know when you're going to meet God."

"Well, Sam," Officer Madison said, "I just asked God to save me. Maybe now we can help each other keep on the right track."

"That'll be great for both of you," Pastor Mike said. "Let me get your names and addresses, and I'll send you the name of a good church nearby. Let me leave these with you." Pastor Mike gave each man a small book. "It's the Gospel of John. Read a little every day. It will help keep you on the right track."

The two men thanked Mike and returned to their car. Gil followed Pastor Mike and Dad back to the truck. Gil listened as Pastor Mike and Dad talked about what had happened. Finally, they stopped talking and Gil spoke up.

"How do you do that, Pastor Mike?"

"Do what?"

"Talk to people like that? Aren't you scared?"

"I don't know if I would call it 'scared.' Nervous, maybe. Why do you ask?"

"I just don't think I could do that—just start telling someone how to be saved."

"You just have to be willing to take the opportunities God gives you. What happened this evening was a God-given opportunity. Officer Madison had obviously heard the gospel before, and that seed had grown in his heart, and he was ready to receive Jesus as his Savior. All I had to do was give him the direction to do it."

"You mean God allowed us to be here when this accident happened so you could talk to those officers?"

"That's exactly what I mean. Even though we'll be getting home later than we had planned, I certainly don't consider that time wasted. Any time we lost was well worth it. Your horse-buying trip turned into a mission trip. You never know how God will work. You just have to follow where He leads."

Chapter 6

"We're here!" Pastor Mike announced as he pulled into Granddad Freeman's gravel driveway.

Gil sat up and rubbed his eyes. "I must have fallen asleep."

"Gil, you've been asleep for at least the last fifty miles." His dad laughed. "Buying a horse wore you out."

"But I'm awake now. Do you think Granddad is still awake?" Gil leaned forward in the seat to look up at the house. "It looks like the light's still on."

"He usually goes to bed early so he can get up early. But it's possible." Dad leaned forward to look. "That looks like his reading lamp, though. He may have read himself to sleep. You'd better just get Rattler settled in the shed as quietly as possible and talk to Granddad in the morning."

Pastor Mike pulled up beside the shed, set the brake, and turned off the motor. "Ready to introduce Rattler to his new home, Gil?"

"I hope it's easier getting him out than it was getting him in."

Rattler whinnied impatiently. He moved restlessly, shaking the trailer with every move. Pastor Mike unlocked the tailgate. At the sound of the lock, Rattler lifted his huge head and whinnied again.

A voice called from the house. "Hello out there. Is that you, Walt? Gil, you out there? Sounds like you got what you went for."

"Sure did, Granddad," Gil called up to the window. "I was going to come up and tell you all about him, but Dad thought you were probably asleep."

"Grandma's asleep, but I haven't made it to bed yet. Been waiting here by the window for you to get home. Took you longer than I thought. Come on up and fill me in."

"We'll be up as soon as we get Rattler out of the trailer," Dad called. "I'm not sure how long that will take us."

"Not too long if you use the right persuasion," Granddad called back.

It turned out to be a lot easier to get Rattler out of the trailer than into it. With just a little bit of coaxing and the smell of some fresh hay, Rattler backed out of the trailer. That was the easy part. Getting him into the shed was another matter altogether.

"Come on, Rattler." Gil tugged on the lead rope. "This is your new home. It's not so bad."

Rattler jerked his head, his eyes wide, his nostrils flaring. Gil held the rope tightly in his hand. "Steady, boy. There's nothing in here to be afraid of."

"I think he disagrees with you there, Gil." Dad reached over to help hold the rope. "It's going to take him some time to get used to things around here. You go get that bucket of feed Tim gave you and see if we can get him in the shed the same way we got him in the trailer."

It took some doing, but Rattler was finally settled in his new stall. He moved restlessly, swinging his head from side to side.

"I know it's not what you're used to." Gil climbed up on a bale of hay. "But there's nothing to be afraid of, really." He patted Rattler's neck. "I do know how you feel, though. I don't like going to new places either. And sometimes I get spooked in the dark too. Dad always calls it the fear of the unknown. He says you just have to trust the One who knows what's next. I guess we both need to learn that part. Maybe we can learn it together."

"That's pretty good advice, Son, even for a horse." Dad put his hand on Gil's shoulder. "You've got your work cut out for you, though."

"I know. It's always easier to tell someone else everything's going to be all right than it is to believe it yourself." Gil smiled up at Dad. "I'm not afraid of a little hard work, though."

"Just act on what you know is true, and with God's help, you'll do it." Dad turned toward the door. "By the way, Pastor Mike asked me to tell you goodbye. He thought he'd better head for home. He wanted me to tell you that he thinks you bought a fine horse."

"I couldn't have gotten Rattler without him." Gil jumped down from the bale of hay. "Let's go tell Granddad all about Rattler."

Gil knew right where Granddad would be when they got up to the house, his wheelchair pulled up to the picture window that overlooked the pastures and the shed. That was Granddad's favorite spot and where he spent most of his time.

"Got back kind of late, didn't you?" Granddad greeted them with a smile. "I thought you'd planned to be back before dark."

"We did, but Al Burgess and his son, Tim, invited us to stay for supper. And then we had quite an adventure on the way home. We'll have to tell you about it. Anyway, it slowed us down just a little."

"Well, I'm just glad you got here when you did. I'm afraid it's too dark for me to see that horse of yours tonight, but from the sound of him, he's quite a piece of horseflesh. He must be a mighty fine animal."

"He is, Granddad. He's smart and strong and . . ."

"I'll be the judge of that when I see him in the daylight. You had some trouble getting him in the shed, didn't you? A little rambunctious maybe?"

"Al Burgess used that word. Is that bad?"

"No, it just means he has a lot more uncontrolled energy than common sense. I hope you remembered everything I taught you about checking out a horse before you bought him. From what I heard, you may have your hands full."

Dad spoke up. "Gil and I both looked him over, and Al filled us in on all his shortcomings. I think Gil's going to learn some valuable lessons from this horse. He's nothing Gil can't handle. Maybe the horse will learn a few lessons from Gil at the same time."

"Well, learning lessons is always good. What did you say the horse's name is?"

"Rattler." Gil watched Granddad's face.

"Sounds tough to me. You sure you can handle this horse?"

"His name's Rattler—not 'cause he acts like one, but because he got bit by one. He may look big and tough, but he's afraid of everything."

"Now that's not too good either. Sounds like you do have your work cut out for you." Granddad wheeled himself toward the hallway. "It's time you headed for home. I'll look over this wonder horse in the morning. You can show him off for me before you start working if you get here at seven in the morning."

"Seven o'clock? But tomorrow's Saturday. Wouldn't nine be okay?" Gil pushed his fingers through his hair. "Buying a horse is hard work."

"I suppose it is. But the earlier you get started, the sooner you'll get done. Come right up to the house and I'll give you your instructions. You be here by seven every Saturday morning starting tomorrow, and I'll make sure you have time for your horse and time to earn that money you owe me."

"Granddad's right. If you're going to get started right, you'd better plan to be over here early."

Gil looked from Dad to Granddad. They aren't kidding, he thought. They really expect me to get up early every Saturday morning. "What about this summer? Am I going to have to get up early on Saturdays then too?"

"We'll talk about that when summer gets here. But for now, don't go fretting about missing your beauty sleep." Granddad always seemed to know what he was thinking. "Getting up early and doing a little hard work never hurt anyone."

"I know, Granddad, it's just that . . ."

"It's just that you didn't quite think this part through." Dad put his hand on Gil's shoulder. "I tried to tell you it would be a lot of hard work to take care of a horse and earn what you need to pay back your granddad. You said you could handle it."

"And I can! I just hadn't counted on getting up so early to do it." Gil rubbed his sneaker back and forth against the carpet.

"Son, you know what you need to do."

"Yes, sir. Granddad, I'll see you bright and early in the morning. I may be half asleep, but I'll be here."

"Just make sure your eyes are open," Granddad's eyes twinkled. "Especially if you're planning to ride your bike over. I'll see you in the morning."

"Sure thing, Granddad."

It was going to be a long time 'til summer.

Chapter 7

Gil's feet hit the floor the minute his alarm clock sounded the next morning. This would be as bad as a school day, he thought, if it weren't for Rattler waiting for him and the fact that jeans and a T-shirt were a lot easier to get into than school clothes. He thought he'd given himself plenty of time, but the minutes were ticking away too fast.

"Don't have time to eat, Mom." He grabbed a banana on his way past the kitchen counter. "Gotta get going. I promised Granddad I'd be there by seven, and I want to check on Rattler before I go up to the house." Gil opened the refrigerator. "Do we have any carrots?"

"For breakfast?"

"No, for Rattler. I thought I'd better take him something to show him I'm his friend. If you don't have any carrots, I could use a sugar cube or two."

"Carrots, I have. Sugar cubes, I don't." Mom reached past Gil and pulled a bag of carrots out of the bottom bin of the refrigerator. "These good enough for your horse?"

"Sure, Mom, thanks." Gil took two big carrots from the bag and stuffed them in his pockets.

"Now what are you going to eat? You'd better at least have a bowl of cereal." Mom set a bowl on the table. "You won't work long on an empty stomach."

"Thanks, Mom. But I'll grab something at Granddad's. Grandma always saves something for me when she knows I'm coming. Besides, it's quarter 'til seven now. I'll have to ride fast to get there on time. You know Granddad, a minute late and you might as well have been an hour late." Gil gave his mom a quick kiss. "Don't worry, I won't starve. And I'll be home in time for supper."

It was a good thing his bike was leaning up against the garage. He wouldn't have had time to get it out. He just couldn't be late his first morning. He could hear Granddad saying, "Gil, punctuality is a sign of strong character. If you're late, you're not only wasting your time, you're wasting everyone else's too." That was Granddad; he never missed an opportunity to teach a lesson. It was funny how it was a little easier to take advice from Granddad than from most other adults. "Granddad just doesn't make me feel dumb, I guess," Gil said out loud to a passing rock.

Less than ten minutes later, Gil slid to a stop beside the shed. He unlatched the door and squinted into the darkness.

"Rattler, it's me, Gil. Good morning, boy," Gil called softly. "How're you doing?"

Rattler turned his head and whinnied.

"That sounds like a good morning to me. I guess nothing jumped out of the dark last night to scare you, did it?" Gil climbed up on the side of the stall and held his hand out to Rattler. The big horse nuzzled the offered hand and then gently pushed against it.

"Oh, I know what you want. A carrot or a lump of sugar. I know you like sugar better, but a carrot is the best I could do today." Gil held the carrot out for Rattler. When it was gone, he stroked the soft nose and traced the white star with his finger. "I'd better go." He looked at his watch. "Looks like I have about thirty seconds to get up to the house. But I'll be back, don't you worry. Soon as Granddad gives me working orders."

Gil could see Granddad already in his place by the window. He ran around the back of the house and let himself in the kitchen door.

"Right on time, I see, Gil," Granddad called.

Gil scooted around the kitchen table and into the living room. "Actually, I'm a minute late. But that's because I stopped to see Rattler."

"I don't blame you for that. Besides, you were on the property by seven, so that counts. I'd worry about you if you didn't stop to see that horse."

"Where's Grandma?"

"She left early to go help out over at the church. They've got some big supper tonight for the Ladies Missionary Society. She'll be back in time to fix us lunch if that's what you're worried about." Granddad's eyes twinkled.

"Me worried about food? Never!" Gil opened his mouth in mock surprise. "But speaking of food, I didn't stop to eat any breakfast. I didn't think I was hungry, but now it feels like my stomach is about to chew through my backbone. I had a banana, but I used all that up riding over here. Could I have a bowl of cereal before I start working?"

"A bowl of cereal? I should say not. Not when your grandmother left some of her special ham biscuits on a plate at the back of the stove. She said for you to eat all you want. Go and get them and pour yourself a tall glass of milk while you're at it. While you're eating, I'll talk."

Gil returned from the kitchen with a biscuit in his mouth, a plate of biscuits in one hand, and a glass of milk in the other.

Granddad laughed. "I guess it's a good thing I'm planning to do most of the talking."

Gil sat on a chair near Granddad.

"First, I want to tell you how proud I am of you. Not many twelve-year-old boys would have done what you did. You set a goal and then carried through to reach that goal. And God has rewarded your diligence with that beautiful horse. But did you notice that He didn't do everything for you? He left you some room for growing too. He doesn't make things too easy."

Gil swallowed. "What do you mean?"

"God could have given you a horse that would require very little training and a minimum of care. Instead, He gave you a horse with a few problems to overcome, one that you'll have to keep an eye on and work with. God wants you to learn some lessons from this horse at the same time the horse is learning lessons from you. Don't you think so?"

Gil took his last swallow of milk. "I don't know. Rattler seems almost perfect to me. He's smart and strong and mostly trained. He's waiting down there in the shed right now just as calm and peaceful as you please."

"He wasn't so peaceful last night when you brought him home. He sounded pretty skittish to me."

"He was scared to death. But it seems like he's afraid only when he doesn't know what's going to happen next."

"You mean, like most people, he's afraid of the unknown?"

"That's what Dad calls it. When he can't see his way or he sees something he doesn't understand, he gets all jumpy."

"Seems to me a certain young man was pretty scared when he had to go to a new school last fall. You were so worried, you almost made yourself sick. But after the year started and you met the other kids and got to know the school, everything was fine. Am I right?"

"I didn't think anybody knew I was scared."

"I prayed for you every day because I knew you were fearful and not trusting."

"But there's nothing wrong with being a little afraid, is there? Doesn't it make you careful?"

"There's a difference between being afraid and being careful."

"But aren't you ever afraid? Like when you found out you were going to be in a wheelchair, weren't you afraid then?"

"Sure I was—until I remembered who was in charge. And I learned a long time ago that when I'm afraid, if I quote a verse of Scripture or sing a song to remind me of how great God is, that feeling goes away. I just have to remind myself that everything is in God's control."

"And you think God gave me a fearful horse so I'd learn to trust Him more?"

"I sure do. There's no better way to learn something than to teach it to someone else. You have to let that horse know who is in control. When he senses that you are there and in control, he will cease to be afraid."

"But what about when I'm not there? Will he still be afraid?"

"Probably. But that's where you and that horse are different. You can't be with him all the time. But God is with you every minute of every day. He never leaves you."

Gil sat for a moment without moving. "I think I understand what you're trying to say." Gil was silent for a moment. "There's still something I don't understand, though."

"What's that, Son?"

"How do you do it?"

"How do I do what?"

"How do you know so much about God and who He is and what He wants us to be? You always seem to know what lesson God's trying to teach. How do you know all that?"

It was Granddad's turn to be silent. Through the open window, Gil heard Rattler nickering. A mourning dove called from a nearby tree.

Granddad laid his hand on the Bible on his knee. "That, Gil, is the work of the Holy Spirit using the Word of God to guide me.

RAMBUNCTIOUS RATTLER

My favorite life-guiding verses are Proverbs 3:5-6, Galatians 2:20, Ephesians 3:20, and Titus 2:11-14. Sometime I'll tell you the whole story of how God has guided and blessed me, including this wheelchair. But right now you've got a horse to feed and chores to do. We'll come back to this another time."

They heard Rattler nicker again.

"What do you want me to do first?"

"The first thing you need to do is feed and groom Rattler and then let him out into the lower pasture to explore and find the creek. I had someone come by the other day to check the fence, and it's all sound. Just check the gate to make sure it's latched."

"What do I do after that?"

"Take a little time to get to know your horse. Starting at nine you can plow up Grandma's garden patch so she can start planting. You can leave the horse in the pasture while you work. By then it will be lunch time, and you're on your own after that. Now get out there and get to know that horse. Just remember, let him know you're in charge and that there's nothing to fear."

"Thanks, Granddad, I will," Gil called over his shoulder as he ran out the door. It was time to go make friends with Rattler.

Chapter 8

Gil prepared the feed for Rattler just like Tim had told him. While Rattler ate, Gil straightened out the shed. He found a place for the saddle, bridle, ropes, combs, brush, and hoof pick Tim had sold him. One thing Dad and Granddad insisted on was "A place for everything and everything in its place." They'd be checking up on him; he was sure of that.

"How about a look outside, big guy?" Gil said. "Looks like you've had about all you can eat for now. I think it's time I show you the rest of this place."

Rattler seemed to nod his head in agreement. He stamped his feet and whinnied.

"All right, all right. Don't rush me. We'll get there soon enough." Gil carefully fitted the bridle into Rattler's mouth and attached the lead rope. "I'll let you take a look around before I ride you. No sense making you get used to me on your back and a new place at the same time."

Gil led Rattler out of the shed into the bright sunlight. The horse lifted his head and shook his mane.

"Feels good to be outside, doesn't it? Don't worry, you won't be spending a lot of time in that shed if I can help it. I'm an outdoors man myself."

Gil unclipped the lead rope. "Go on now, take a look around. When you've seen enough, come right back here. When you get back, we'll see about a little bareback riding."

The spot where Gil stood overlooked Granddad's three acres of woods and pastureland. A gurgling creek flowed on the far edge of the lower pasture. Along the top of the hill near Granddad's house were some picnic tables under three big oak trees. What a perfect place to keep a horse. The whole three acres was fenced on three sides, and the creek formed the boundary for the lower pasture so that Rattler would have plenty of water. I couldn't have planned it better myself, Gil thought. Mom can sit up there at those picnic tables and watch me ride sometime.

Just then Rattler came up over the rise in the pasture. His hooves pounded as he raced up the hill. As he neared Gil, he slowed to a walk.

"Well, what do you think? Do you think you'll like it here?"

Again, Rattler shook his head as if to say yes. "Hey, that's pretty good. I thought in the shed it was just a fluke. I guess you're used to Tim talking to you. I'm sure you don't really understand what I'm saying, but you sure seem to. Rattler, you just get better and better."

Gil dropped the lead rope over the gate. He grabbed the bridle and led Rattler near the fence. "Time to ride," he said as he climbed onto Rattler's back. With a leap, Rattler was off across the pasture.

Gil used the reins to guide him to the path in the woods that would take them to the lower pasture. As they neared the woods, however, Rattler reared, and Gil slid to the ground.

"Those woods look pretty spooky, huh? I guess since you got bit once, you think every time you come to woods you're going to get bit again. Well, I'll just walk you through a few times and show you there's nothing to worry about. Then maybe next time you won't dump me when we get here."

Gil grabbed the bridle and led Rattler down the path. When they came to the lower pasture, Gil jumped on his back again.

They rode hard to the far side of the pasture where the honey-suckle vines were entwined in the fence. Suddenly, Rattler reared again, dumping Gil to the ground. This time Rattler did not stay but galloped in the direction of the picnic area. Gil ran after him and finally caught up. Rattler stood trembling with his nostrils flared. Gil grabbed the bridle.

"If you keep this up, I'm going to have to put a saddle on you. It's no fun getting dumped without warning. And I can't hang on without a saddle. What in the world scared you anyway? Was there a snake down there too?" Gil searched the landscape.

"I think he smells a bear," Granddad called from the window above their heads.

"A bear? Here?"

"Well, not here yet, but close by. You and Rattler are down-wind from him. That horse must have picked up the bear's scent from the wind, and that's what spooked him. He sensed the danger."

"But I don't see any bear."

"You can't see him from down there. Remember, I have binoculars. I was looking up toward the mountains with my binoculars and saw the bear coming down this way. Not many black bears are seen in these parts. Black bears can roam over fifty miles in twenty-four hours. This one must be looking for food."

"Do you think he'll come all the way down here?"

"I can't be sure. If he's hungry, there's no telling what he'll do. Bears don't usually bother horses, but horses have a healthy fear of them. Bears, however, have been known to attack humans. If he comes across that creek, you come in immediately. I can still see him, and he's definitely coming this way."

Gil held the bridle and tried to calm Rattler. He couldn't see the bear yet, but he knew Granddad was keeping him in sight with his binoculars. Soon Gil could hear a rustling in the woods and field across the creek. It wasn't long before he saw a black nose poke through the brush.

"There he is, Rattler. But you're safe with me. Or I'm safe with you. I'm not sure which. There's no food up here, so I don't think he'll come across the creek."

"He's looking for blackberries down there," Granddad said from the window. "They're not ripe yet, so he won't find any to eat."

The bear turned from the berry bushes to a large tree in the far corner of the field beyond the creek.

"That's a bee tree, and he hears the bees. I don't think he'll find much honey though. Not this time of year."

The bear turned and left the way he came. Gil heaved a sigh of relief.

"I think he's gone, Granddad."

"Looks like he's leaving, all right. But he may be back in a few months looking for those blackberries."

"I'm sure glad you could see all that. I could make out the bear, but I didn't know what he was up to. Rattler and I were plenty scared."

"He'll be fine as soon as the scent of the bear is gone. Are you all right?"

"Sure, I was fine as soon as I saw him leaving. I'd just never seen a bear come this close before."

"They don't do it often. But when they do, you have to be careful."

After Rattler calmed down, Gil mounted him again and walked him over the open pasture. "See, Rattler, there's not much here that can hurt a horse." Rattler broke into a trot. "You must be feeling better. Okay, let's go!" They galloped at full speed around the pasture.

As they came to a stop near the fence, the whine of a chain saw erupted from the woods that bordered the property. Up went Rattler and down went Gil.

"That does it. From now on I'm using the saddle. That's just a chain saw, and it's far enough away that we can't even see it, so I doubt it's going to hurt you."

Gil took off the bridle and left the halter on. "I don't know about you, but I've had enough for right now. No offense, Rattler. You're a great horse, but it's awful hard to stay on you without a saddle, and the way you're acting, I don't think a saddle would make you too happy." Gil rubbed Rattler's nose. "You've just got to stop being such a fraidy cat. Dad says 'You can't go through life being afraid of everything.' Tell you what. You just walk around the pasture for a while, and if you feel like rearing, you can do it without dumping me on the ground. I have to go till up Grandma's garden anyway. I have to make some money to finish paying for you. Now don't get me wrong. In spite of three spills in one morning, I still think you're worth it." Gil patted Rattler's broad back. "Go on now, explore, but don't get out of the fence."

Gil made sure the latch was closed on the pasture gate. He headed up behind the house to find the tiller and get started on the garden.

"Granddad's right," he said to himself. "I do have my work cut out for me—in more ways than one."

Chapter 9

After lunch Gil said goodbye to Granddad and headed over to Billy's house. He couldn't wait to tell him about Rattler. He knew Billy had been disappointed when he couldn't go with them to get the horse. It was rough for a twelve year old to have to be the man of the house, but ever since his dad had died, Billy spent his spare time doing odd jobs to help out. Yesterday he had taken over Gil's paper route so Gil could go to Georgia.

Billy was just getting ready to start the mower when Gil came around the corner of the house.

"Hey, Billy, wait." Gil ran around to where Billy could see him.

"Hey, Gil, I didn't see you coming." Billy grinned. "Did you get that horse?"

"Sure did. He's a beaut. I came by to see if you could come over and see him."

"Wish I could. I promised Mom I'd have the yard mowed before she got home from work. And you know what that means, all the trimming and weeding too. She says the job's not done until you've finished all the trim work. I don't mind usually, but I'd sure like to see that horse."

"Tell you what, I'll help you. You run the mower and I'll do the weeding. Between the two of us we ought to be done in half the time. When we're done, we'll leave a note for your mom telling her that you're with me at my granddad's. That way if she gets home early she won't worry."

"She's usually home by four on Saturdays, so that doesn't give us much time. Let's get going."

The boys had the yard finished in no time. After careful inspection, Billy announced he thought it would meet his mother's approval. "She always insists that our yard be 'above reproach,' as she puts it." Billy wiped his forehead. "She says she doesn't want anyone to accuse us of bringing down the neighborhood just 'cause we're black. Like we're not good enough to live here. I just hate it when she says things like that. But it's true. People think that just because our skin's different we're not going to be good neighbors. It just makes me so mad."

"I know, Billy. But you know I don't care what color you are, and Rattler won't either. Let's get going."

The boys grabbed their bikes and headed back to Granddad's house. As they rode up to the house, they could see Rattler standing in the shade of one of the oak trees.

"Wow, he's something to see, isn't he? What a horse!"

"Isn't he great? I can't believe he's mine." Gil leaned his bike against the house. "Go on down to the gate. I'll be right there. I just want to tell Granddad we're here."

Gil returned with some carrots in his hand. "Here. If you feed him one of these, he'll be your friend for life."

Rattler welcomed them with a soft whinny. Billy held out his carrot, keeping his hand flat. Very carefully Rattler took it from him. "Whew!" Billy whistled softly. "He's great!"

"He sure is." Gil fed Rattler a second carrot. "He has his problems, though."

"I don't see anything wrong with him."

"You can't see it just by looking. One problem he has is a limp. It's only a slight one. Most people don't notice it when he walks. But that's why the owner was selling him. He's no good as a show horse with that limp."

"What else is wrong with him?"

"He's a spooker."

"A spooker?"

"Yeah, he's afraid of just about everything. Ever since he got bit by a rattler, he's been afraid of everything."

"He didn't seem to be afraid of me."

"That's because you didn't make any sudden moves. If he's not sure what's going to happen next or something startles him, he spooks."

"Well, I guess nobody's perfect."

"Nope, and Granddad says the Lord let me get a horse with a few problems so I could learn some lessons too."

"Your granddad always says God had something to do with everything. I just can't see that if there is a God, He would care what kind of horse you got. He didn't care enough about me to let my dad live."

"Billy, you know that's not true. God cares about every detail of our lives. Your dad is in heaven, and you can see him again if you trust Christ as your Savior."

"I know. My mom keeps telling me I need to get saved so I can see my dad again."

"Well, that's not the only reason you need to get saved."

"I know, I know. I've heard it all before. Let's not talk about that now. I came to see your horse, not to get preached at. Can I ride him?"

"Maybe sometime. But we'd probably better not try to saddle him up right now. He got spooked by a bear earlier and then a chain saw."

"A bear?"

"Granddad said it was a black bear that had come down from the mountains looking for food."

"Bet that scared Rattler."

"Yeah, and me too, for a while. It looked like he was going to come right across the creek."

"He wouldn't have come this far, though, would he?"

"I don't know. All I know is Granddad sure knows a lot about everything. He knew all about black bears and was telling me stuff about them while the bear was coming this way."

"Boys," Grandma called from the window. "Billy's mother just called to make sure Billy was here, and I invited her to come for dinner. I thought we could cook outside so we can all enjoy watching Rattler. Gil, I called your folks, too, and they said for you to stay here until then."

"Thanks, Grandma. That sounds great. Is there anything we can do to help?"

"I'm sure I can find something for you boys to do. Come on up, and we'll see what needs to be done."

Gil and Billy spent the next few minutes preparing the fire and sweeping off the picnic table. They carried down supplies and helped set the table. When everything was ready, Gil wheeled Granddad down from the house.

"It's a perfect day for a cookout, don't you think, Gil?"

"It sure is, Granddad. I'm glad Grandma thought of it."

"Well, you know your grandmother—she takes every opportunity to be hospitable. She has the gift of hospitality."

"I'm sure glad she has it." Gil grinned and rubbed his stomach. "If hospitality involves food, I'm all for it."

"Me too." Billy helped Gil get Granddad's wheelchair up to a picnic table.

By the time Billy's mom and Gil's parents arrived, the grilled chicken was done to perfection. Gil carried down the last dish from the refrigerator, a huge bowl of potato salad. He managed to squeeze it between the sliced tomatoes, pickles, baked beans, and fruit salad. What a feast!

Granddad asked the blessing. "Lord, we thank You today for Your bountiful provision of food. We thank You for friends old and new. And we thank You for the fine new horse you've allowed Gil to buy. May we glorify Your name in all we do and say this evening. In Jesus' name, Amen."

"Let's eat." Gil eyed the chicken and licked his lips.

"Guests first, Son." Gil's dad passed the chicken to Mrs. Grishom. "You and Billy just start whatever's nearest to you."

Gil and Billy filled their plates with everything within reach and then added the chicken. In a matter of minutes their plates were clean and ready for seconds.

"You boys really worked up an appetite today, didn't you?" Mrs. Grishom smiled at Billy. "I saw the good job you did on the yard. I sure appreciate your helping Billy, Gil."

"How'd you know I did?"

"Billy mentioned it in the note he left me. That's a lot of yard to take care of and is almost more than Billy can do alone, so he's always glad to get some help."

"No problem, Mrs. Grishom. I never mind helping a friend."

Rattler whinnied from his place near the shed.

"I think that fine animal of yours is getting hungry," Granddad said. "As soon as you're done here, you'd better give him his supper."

"Sure thing, Granddad. Billy can help me."

"That's what friends are for." Billy slapped Gil on the back. "What's a little work between friends?"

"If you fellows hurry, I'll tell you an old Indian tale about the friendship between a horse and a rabbit. I think you'll like it."

"And while your granddad's telling his story, you can roast some marshmallows over what remains of the fire." Grandma pulled a bag of marshmallows out of the picnic basket she had carried down. "Walt, do you have your knife on you?"

"Sure do, Mom. What do you need it for?"

"Cut those boys some branches to roast the marshmallows the old-fashioned way."

By the time Gil and Billy had fed and watered Rattler and put him in his stall, the fire was just right for roasting marshmallows. One after the other, the white pillows of sugar turned golden brown as Granddad told his story.

"It was the time of year during those beautiful autumn days called Indian summer when the trees were turning bright red and deep rich orange brown. The weather, which had been pretty nippy in the mornings, would turn warm by the afternoon. On such afternoons a fine Indian pony—we'll call him Paint—loved to take a nap. Sometimes he slept standing up; but when a cool breeze was blowing, he would go behind the big rock in his pasture and lie down and soak up the warm sunshine.

"It was on one such afternoon, when the cool breeze chilled the warm afternoon, that Paint stretched out behind his rock in the sun-drenched clover for an afternoon snooze. After about an hour he woke up, startled. There against his stomach was a white ball of fur. He was about to jerk up and run when a head popped up out of that ball of fur, and Paint saw that it was a rabbit. Paint calmed down. The rabbit was so small he knew it could not hurt him.

"The rabbit was afraid too. He had been out in the middle of the pasture far away from the entrance to his underground burrow when he saw a hawk circling, ready to dive and snatch him up. The entrance to the burrow was too far away, but then the rabbit saw the horse. He ran quickly to the horse and snuggled up against him. He knew the hawk would not dive at such a large animal. He was afraid, however, that when the horse woke up he might stand up and step on him.

"Paint saw the hawk circling overhead. He knew the rabbit was hiding from this fearsome predator. Very cautiously, he stood up. As the rabbit moved toward its burrow, Paint walked carefully with him, protecting him from the hawk. When they reached the burrow, the rabbit disappeared inside.

"Paint waited, hoping the rabbit would return. The rabbit did return and brought with him another rabbit. The two rabbits looked at Paint as if to say thank you.

"Then they did a very strange thing. They hopped to a nearby rock and climbed to the top of it. And then they waited. Paint moved closer to the rock, wondering what the rabbits wanted him to do. When he was close enough to them, the rabbits jumped from the rock to Paint's back. This startled Paint. He was used to having a human on his back but never an animal. He started galloping right away and the two rabbits rode on his back in grand style. He finally slowed to a walk and then took the rabbits back to the rock where they had started. During the next weeks Paint returned to the rock each day and waited. Before long, the rabbits would appear, and Paint would give them a ride around the pasture.

"One day Paint's Indian rider observed this unusual friendship. He called his friends to see the wonderful sight of the rabbits riding on the horse's back. Never had they seen such an example of friendship."

Gil poked the last bit of marshmallow into his mouth. "Aw, horses and rabbits don't really act like that."

"It's an old Indian legend, Gil, and the Indians believed it was true. What it does show us is how people or animals who are very different can become friends and help each other. We should never say, 'I can't be that person's friend because he's different than I am.' If God gives us the opportunity to be friends with someone, we should make the most of it. God wants us to love and help each other."

Billy moved restlessly next to Gil. "Yeah, but sometimes people don't want to be friends with me."

"Then you have to be as kind as you can be and show them that you're the same as they are inside." Granddad patted the arm of his wheelchair. "I know how you feel, though. This chair makes many people uncomfortable. But I can't let that stop me from being friendly."

"Maybe. But I find it real hard to be nice to people who aren't nice to me just because I'm a different color."

"Don't let that keep you from finding friends, though, Billy. Besides, God doesn't care what color our skin is. He's concerned about our hearts." Granddad leaned toward Billy. "How *is* your heart, Billy?"

"Okay, I guess." Billy threw his stick on the ground and began picking up the trash. He carried what he could to some distance away.

"I'm sorry, Mr. Freeman." Mrs. Grishom stood up from the table. "Billy doesn't want to talk about his heart. Since his dad died, he feels like God doesn't care. I thank the Lord every day that He brought us to Greendale. Billy's friendship with Gil is probably the only thing that's keeping him from getting into trouble."

"We'll keep praying for him. He'll come to see the truth someday. We'll pray that it will be soon."

After the table was cleared and the fire put out, Gil helped Billy load his bike into the trunk of his mother's car.

"I'll see you tomorrow." Gil dusted off his hands.

"I don't know. I may sleep late in the morning." Billy wouldn't look in Gil's direction.

"Oh, come on, Billy; don't quit on me now. We've been going to Sunday school for a long time together. You can't stay home now."

"I don't know. I'll see. Mom'll probably make me go, anyway. Guess I'll see you tomorrow." Billy got in the car.

"See you, Billy."

The taillights disappeared down the driveway.

You can't tell by looking at Rattler that he's a spooker, and you can't tell by looking at Billy that he's not saved. Looks like I have my work cut out for me on both accounts, thought Gil. He waved a final goodbye and turned toward the house.

Chapter 10

Gil did not see much of Billy over the next few weeks. Between taking care of Rattler, going to school, keeping up with his chores, and doing homework, there wasn't much time. Occasionally, Gil passed Billy at school or as they ran their paper routes, but there wasn't much time for talking then. Gil kept praying for Billy, asking God to give him another chance to talk to him about his soul.

The first Saturday after school got out, Gil finished his work at Granddad's early. He rode by Billy's house to see if he was home. Billy was just finishing the yard work his mom had asked him to do.

"Hey, Billy." Gil slid his bike to a stop on the cement driveway. "What you been up to? Haven't seen much of you lately."

"Just been busy, I guess." Billy wound the hose onto its rack. "How's that horse of yours doing these days?"

"He's doing great." Gil laid down his bike and walked over to where Billy stood. "That's why I'm here. I wondered if you wanted to ride over to Granddad's with me to see him. I thought between the two of us, we'd give him some good exercise."

Billy wiped his hands on his jeans. "That sounds great. Hang on, and I'll go ask my mom."

Billy returned with his hands washed and his shirttail tucked in. "Mom said I could go as long as I didn't look like a hoodlum, whatever that means."

Gil laughed. "Yeah, my mom says things like that too; though why you need to tuck your shirttail in to go see a horse is beyond me. Oh well, let's go."

Rattler was nowhere to be seen when they rode up the lane to the pasture.

"That's strange." Gil stopped and scanned the pasture. "I can usually see him from here."

The boys rode on up to the gate. The latch had been lifted, and the gate stood open.

"Looks like Rattler made a break for freedom!" Billy stopped his bike next to the open gate. "I wonder how long he's been gone."

Gil dropped his bike and examined the latch. "I don't know. But he must have opened this himself. I'm going to run up to the house to see if Granddad saw anything."

"I'll come with you."

The boys left their bikes by the gate and ran to the house. Without even stopping to knock, Gil ran in the back door.

"Granddad! Granddad! Rattler's gone!"

"Whoa, slow down there, Gil. Rattler's gone?" Granddad looked up from the book he was reading.

"The gate's open and he's gone!" Billy ran in behind Gil. "We came over to ride him. And he's gone."

"Now calm down a minute. Catch your breath, both of you. You say the gate was open?" Granddad closed the book and laid it on the table. He wheeled himself to the window and picked up his binoculars. He scanned the pasture first, then looked toward the gate. "He doesn't seem to be out there anywhere. And the gate is open. Did you latch it when you left?"

"Sure I did. I always make sure it's latched tightly. Tim warned me about Rattler getting out."

Granddad turned his chair back to face the boys. "Do you suppose Rattler's been watching you open that gate enough to know how to lift that latch?"

"He does sometimes come to the gate when I leave. I never thought about his watching me open and close the gate, but that's how Tim said he learned to lift the latch at the horse farm. If he sees it done often enough, he imitates what he sees. I should have known better."

"You were as careful as you could be. What you need to focus on now is finding that horse before he gets into any real mischief." Granddad patted the arm of his chair. "If it weren't for this contraption, I'd get right out there with you. But I'll be here praying that the Lord will direct your steps. Now get going. You've got to find him before it gets dark."

"But which way do we go?" Gil scratched his head.

"When you get to the end of the lane, check the soft dirt there. You should be able to tell which way his tracks go. Be sure to take a rope to tie on the halter. You'll need a way to lead him home."

Gil ran to the shed and grabbed the rope. The two boys wasted no time getting back to their bikes and riding to the end of the lane. Sure enough, there in the soft dirt were Rattler's tracks, leading toward town.

"I sure hope he hasn't gotten too far." Gil pushed off down the road. Billy was not far behind.

They had not ridden too far when they heard a whinny.

"Over there." Gil pointed in the direction of a neighbor's house. "That sounded like Rattler over there."

The neighbor's driveway wound back through the trees and then opened up at the house. On one side of the house was a beautiful garden patch. Standing in the middle of the garden patch was

Rattler. A woman stood on the porch of the house waving her apron and shouting.

"You get out of my garden! You're trampling everything!"

Gil ran toward the horse. "Rattler, come out of there. Can't you see you're ruining this lady's garden?"

Rattler lifted his head, looked at Gil, and returned to eating the carrot tops.

"Young man, is that your horse?"

"Yes, ma'am. He opened the gate and got out."

"Well, you'd better get him out of my garden before he does any more damage, or you'll have a price to pay."

Gil began moving toward Rattler. He didn't want to spook him. He motioned for Billy to move around the other side. Suddenly, a white sheet on a nearby clothesline snapped in the wind. Rattler bolted around the back of the house. Gil and Billy ran after him.

Behind the house was an in-ground swimming pool. Even though it was the beginning of summer, the black winter cover was still in place. After Rattler ran around the house, he stopped abruptly at the edge of the pool. His nostrils were flared and his eyes wide.

"Easy, Rattler. Easy, boy." Gil approached him cautiously. "It's okay, boy. I'm here to take you home."

Just as Gil got close enough to lay his hands on Rattler's flank, the lady came around the corner of the house.

"Oh, no! Not my swimming pool!"

At that moment, Rattler, startled at the woman's shrill voice, leaped onto the black cover of the pool. It buckled under him and sank to the bottom. There stood Rattler in four feet of water, wide-eyed and frightened. He scrambled frantically for a way out, going from side to side, but his hooves slipped on the tiles.

Gil and Billy ran to the end of the pool where Rattler was making his frantic efforts.

"Easy now. Rattler, it's me, Gil, and Billy. You remember Billy. Just take it easy now. We'll find a way to get you out. But you've got to calm down. There now, just stand still. We'll get you out."

Rattler, calmed by Gil's voice, stopped struggling and stood still. Billy ran back to the bikes to get the rope while Gil continued to talk to Rattler.

"Now what are you boys going to do?" The lady of the house glared at Gil from the side of the pool. "Not only has your horse eaten the tops off all my young carrots, he's ruined the pool cover."

"I'm sorry, ma'am. He just got spooked. I guess he thought the pool cover was solid."

"Do you know how much one of those pool covers costs?"

"No, ma'am, but I'll find out, and I'll get you a new one if it takes me all summer to earn the money for it." Gil wished the woman would go back inside. The sound of her voice seemed to terrify Rattler. "We'll get him out of here just as fast as we can."

Gil was glad to see the woman turn and go back into the house. He'd never get Rattler calmed down as long as she was shouting.

Billy returned with the rope. "Here you go, Gil." He handed the rope to Gil. "How're you going to get him out of there?"

"I'm not. *We* are."

"We? I don't know anything about getting horses out of swimming pools."

"Well, I don't either, but between the two of us I think we can manage. Now look around and see if you can find some boards or something we can lay down for him to step on. Right here near the stairs there's no water, so maybe we can make him a dry place to climb out."

Piled near the pool was some old lumber, boards of many different sizes. Billy found some to lay on the bottom of the pool near the stairs and then some to put on the stairs.

"It's a good thing this pool has long built-in stairs instead of a ladder or we'd never get him out."

"You're right about that. Are you ready?" Gil checked to make sure the rope was tied to the halter. "This is as calm as he's going to get, I think."

Gil led Rattler across the boards and up the steps that Billy had covered with wood. He tied Rattler to a nearby tree and helped Billy get the boards out of the pool.

"I'll go tell the lady we're getting out of her way. I hope she's not too mad." Gil left Billy with Rattler and knocked on the back door of the house. The door opened immediately.

"What's your name, Son?"

"Gil, ma'am."

"Gil what?"

"Gil Freeman. My grandparents live just up the road. I board my horse at their place."

"Yes, I know the Freemans. I must say, you boys did as fine a job of getting that horse out of that pool as two grown men could have done. I'm Mrs. Mansfield." She smiled at Gil. "I watched you from my kitchen window. I had no idea how you were going to manage, but I think you did a great job."

"Thank you, ma'am. And now about the carrots and the pool cover." Gil shifted his weight from one foot to the other.

"As far as the carrots are concerned, you may come back next week and plant two new rows for me. That will settle that. And as far as the pool cover is concerned, I will speak to my husband, of course, but I feel that it was our fault your horse got in the pool, anyway. We should have a fence around that pool. We've been meaning to for years and just never got around to it. If my husband agrees, we'll bear the cost of the pool cover because I'm thankful it was your great big horse that fell in there and not some child who could have drowned."

Gil didn't know what to say. He opened his mouth, but nothing came out.

The woman handed him a bag of cookies. "Here, take these with you. I know you probably need to get that horse home, or I'd ask you to come in for some cookies and milk. So take those along with you and take good care of that horse. He's a fine one."

"Thank you. I'll do that. And I'll be back as soon as I can to replant your carrots."

"That's fine, Son. Now you just run on home with your horse."

Gil showed the cookies to Billy.

"Boy, this sure isn't what I thought you'd get out of this mess. I thought she'd still be mad." Billy helped himself to a cookie.

"Yeah, me too. I guess she was watching us out of the window and saw we were going to take care of the problem. Of course, I was praying hard that God would help me know what to do." Gil untied Rattler from the tree. "I know one thing. I'm wiring that gate shut as soon as I get back to Grandad's, and it's going to stay wired shut from now on. Rattler is not going to lead me into an adventure like this again. Now I know what Granddad meant when he called Rattler 'rambunctious.'"

Chapter 11

Before Gil knew it, the time had come for Billy and him to go to camp for a couple of weeks. They had done this every summer for the last few years, and this summer was to be no exception. But having Rattler meant that this time Gil had to make some preparations before leaving.

"Maybe I should stay home and take care of Rattler for you." Billy kicked at the big tree in the pasture. "That way you'd know he was being well taken care of."

"You know, I thought about not going myself, Billy. But I knew if I didn't go, you wouldn't go either. And since I'm going, you need to also. What's the matter with you, anyway? How come you don't want to go this year? I've got a horse to worry about, but you don't have any reason not to want to go." Gil slid off Rattler and sat down under the tree.

"I don't know. I guess I'm just tired of hearing the same messages over and over again. I've heard it all before, and I don't want to hear it again." Billy flopped down beside Gil. "If I could just go and have fun, it'd be different."

"The messages aren't the problem, Billy. You need to get your heart right, and then you'd want to hear those messages. Why don't you just give in and admit you need to be saved?"

"But that's just it. I don't need to be saved. I'm a good person. I obey my mom and do what I'm told at school. I don't steal, lie, or cheat. So why do I need to be saved? Besides, if God loves me so much, why did He let my dad die?" Billy rolled away from Gil.

For a long time Gil was silent. He and Billy had had this conversation so many times, and it never seemed to be any different. He just didn't know what to say.

"Billy, we've been through all this before. You know without my telling you that your dad's death has nothing to do with whether or not God loves you. I don't know why your dad died when he did. But I do know God loved you enough to send His Son to die on the cross for you, and He freely offers you salvation from sin. And even though you don't do all those bad things that other people do, you're still a sinner because we are all sinners since Adam sinned. You just have to believe and be saved."

"Yeah, I know, I know. It's not that I don't want to. It's just that it never seems like the right time. So let's just drop it, okay? I'll go to camp 'cause you want me to. And I'll listen to all those messages 'cause you want me to. But now you have to find someone else to take care of this horse." Billy stood up and brushed the grass off his jeans. "Got anybody in mind?"

"Sure do. Pastor Mike said he'd be glad to stop by and check on Rattler. He even said that if he had the chance, he'd bring Rattler and his two horses up to camp so the campers could ride them. He didn't promise, but he offered."

Just a few days after the boys arrived at camp, Pastor Mike pulled in with his horse trailer. Billy and Gil were on the steps to meet him.

"Aren't you fellows supposed to be at some activity or something?" Pastor Mike ruffled their hair. "I didn't think you had much free time for just loafing around." He laughed.

"Dad called to let us know you were coming, so we got special permission to meet you and the horses, sir." Gil stood at attention and saluted. "We have our orders to show you the pasture where they will be kept during their stay here, sir."

Pastor Mike smiled and returned Gil's salute. "If that doesn't sound official, I don't know what does. Lead the way, boys."

Gil and Billy hopped in the truck and pointed the way to where the horses would be staying. The boys helped Pastor Mike turn the horses into the pasture.

"There's not much grass here." Billy leaned on the fence.

"That's okay, Billy; I've got it covered." Pastor Mike pulled a bale of hay from the trailer. "There's enough to last them for the few days they'll be up here."

Pastor Mike stayed for supper and then left for home. Under the supervision of their counselor, Gil and Billy were given the responsibility of taking care of the three horses.

Gil got up early the next morning to check on them. He didn't bother Billy. He wanted some time alone with Rattler. When he arrived at the pasture, the three horses were at the far end of the fence. Their nostrils were flaring, and they looked scared to death. After trying to calm them down, he ran to get some help.

"They were really scared of something." Gil filled in Derek, his counselor, and Billy as they walked back down to the pasture. "I tried talking to them and getting them to come eat some hay. But they didn't seem interested. Maybe you can help me figure out what scared them."

The horses were still huddled at the far end of the pasture. Derek, Gil, and Billy did a quick survey of the area.

"Hey, guys, come look at this." Derek called Gil and Billy over. "I think I found out what's scaring those horses." He pointed to the ground. "See these tracks? Those are the tracks of a mountain lion. I had heard there was one in the area, which is very unusual, but to the best of my knowledge this is the first time anyone has seen any tracks."

"Do mountain lions attack horses?" Gil crouched to take a closer look at the tracks.

"Not usually, at least not as far as I know. They often attack young deer and maybe wounded cattle, but I've never heard of one jumping a horse. But it's no wonder those horses are scared."

Billy looked from the tracks to the horses. "I thought cougars were the ones that attacked farm animals."

"Mountain lions often go by other names like cougar and puma. They are the hardest predator to spot too. These tracks are probably all we'll ever see of this mountain lion. They prefer to sleep in the trees and seldom come down to the ground during the day. He's probably just passing through. I don't think he'll bother them again."

The next day Gil, Billy, and Derek took the horses for an early morning ride. They were going up a steep mountain path when something in the underbrush moved, and Rattler reared. Gil pulled hard on the reins and managed to stay on Rattler's back. The frightened horse struck his leg against a sharp rock, cutting a gash that began to bleed profusely.

Gil jumped off Rattler's back. He tried to stop the flow of blood with his hand, but it was coming too fast. "I need something to stop the blood. Give me something, quick!"

"Is he going to bleed to death?" Billy sounded frightened.

Derek crouched down beside Gil. "Not if we can help it, Billy. Here, Gil, let me give you a hand." Derek opened his backpack and pulled out a first-aid kit. "There are bandages in here. I just hope there are enough."

Working together, Derek and Gil were able to place bandages along the gash and then secure them with rolls of gauze. Derek then wrapped the area securely with an elastic bandage.

"That should hold it until we can get him down to a vet. The way that thing was bleeding, I thought he'd be gone before we could get it stopped." Derek motioned for Billy to bring the other horses over. "Gil, you and Billy ride down, and I'll lead Rattler. When you get to camp, call the vet and let him know we're bringing Rattler in."

The vet was at the camp by the time Derek led Rattler back to the pasture.

"That was quick thinking out there, boys." The vet patted Gil and Billy on the back.

"If Derek hadn't had that first-aid kit, I don't know what we would have done. Thanks to him, Rattler's going to be all right."

Gil called Pastor Mike that afternoon and told him what had happened.

"You might as well come on up and get the horses. No one is going to be riding Rattler for a long time. His leg needs time to heal. And if we take the other two out without him, he'll be unhappy."

When Pastor Mike arrived the next day, he examined Rattler's bandages. "I had no idea it was this bad. When you told me on the phone he had been cut, I wasn't picturing anything this big."

"Do you think the Lord's trying to teach me something, Pastor Mike?"

"Like what, Gil?"

"Like maybe I'd better not get too attached to this horse because he won't always be here."

"That is something to consider, Gil." Pastor Mike put his arm around Gil's shoulders. "Do you think maybe Rattler was becoming just a little too important to you?"

"I did think about not coming to camp this year so I could stay home and take care of him. But I knew that if I didn't come, then Billy wouldn't come. And Billy needs to be here. I'm praying that this will be the year he accepts Christ as his personal Savior. Do you think he will?"

"It's hard to say, Gil. Billy's heard the gospel many, many times, and he's rejected it all those times too. I don't know what it will take to reach him. But I'll pray with you that something will get through to him these last few days of camp."

"Thanks, Pastor Mike. Take good care of Rattler for me. See you soon."

Gil walked back up the trail to camp. He wondered where Billy was. He had expected him to go with him to meet Pastor Mike, but when he was ready to go, Billy was nowhere to be found. Gil turned down toward the lake just in case Billy had gone there to be by himself. He'd been doing that a lot lately.

As Gil neared the swimming area, he saw Billy sitting at the end of the pier. Gil called to him.

"Billy, come on up. It's almost time for supper."

Billy did not even lift his head.

Gil tried again. "Billy, you better hurry. You know Derek doesn't like for us to be late for meals."

Still Billy did not turn around. Gil walked on down the hill and out to the end of the pier.

"Hey, Billy. What's the matter? Didn't you hear me?"

Billy looked up at Gil. Gil couldn't believe it—Billy had been crying. He had tried to make it look like he hadn't been. But Gil could tell. He sat down next to Billy.

"You want to tell me about it?"

"About what?"

"About what's on your mind."

"Nothin's on my mind."

"Come on, Billy; you can't fool me. I'm your best friend. I know something's bothering you, and I want you to tell me what it is."

"All right. I'm scared."

"Scared of what?"

"Scared of dying."

"What brought this on?"

"Up there on that mountain, when Rattler got hurt, there was blood everywhere. And I know it wasn't a person, but just the thought of anybody dying right there in front of me scared me to death. I couldn't even pray for you or Rattler or Derek. I couldn't ask God to help you because I have no right to ask God anything, and that scared me too. I felt so helpless. So when I got back to camp, I came out here to think."

"You've been out here since lunch?"

"Just about. When everyone else came to swim, I scrammed into the woods for a while. I bet Derek's really mad 'cause he can't find me. But I needed some time to think."

"And now that you've thought, what have you decided?"

"I've decided I need to quit playing games. Gil, I want to accept Jesus as my Savior. I've known I needed to for a long time, but I didn't want everyone telling me what to do. All those messages I told you I didn't want to hear have all told me the same things you and Mom and Pastor Mike have been telling me. I need to be saved. Can you help me?"

Gil wanted to shout. "Of course I can help you. I've been praying for this moment all summer."

Gil took Billy back through the verses they had learned in Sunday school:

Romans 3:23: For all have sinned, and come short of the glory of God.

Romans 6:23: For the wages of sin is death; but the gift of God is eternal life through Jesus Christ our Lord.

Romans 5:8: But God commendeth his love toward us, in that, while we were yet sinners, Christ died for us.

Romans 10:9: That if thou shalt confess with thy mouth the Lord Jesus, and shalt believe in thine heart that God hath raised him from the dead, thou shalt be saved.

Romans 10:13: For whosoever shall call upon the name of the Lord shall be saved.

RAMBUNCTIOUS RATTLER

Gil knew that Billy knew the verses, but he went through them all again to make sure he understood. When they rose from the end of the pier, Billy was no longer afraid.

Chapter 12

"Gil," Granddad called from the living room. "Can you come here a minute? I think you'd better see this."

Gil set his empty glass in the sink. Grandma smiled at him. "He must have found something interesting in the newspaper. He's always calling me from the kitchen while I'm cooking, wanting me to listen to this or that." She handed him a cookie. "Go on in. But make sure he knows you need to get on home for supper. He loses track of time when he's reading the paper. We don't want you to keep your family waiting."

Gil stepped into the living room. "What is it, Granddad? What did you want me to see?"

"This article about a mystery horse." Granddad handed him the paper. "There in the lower right-hand corner. See it?"

Gil folded the paper in half and began to read.

" 'Late Tuesday afternoon, a horse was seen eating vegetables behind Charlie Snow's Diner. An employee of the diner found the horse eating carrots and other vegetables that had been delivered to the back entrance of the diner. Several boxes had been pushed over and broken. The employee of the diner said that the horse had probably pushed the boxes over while trying to reach a box of apples near the bottom of the stack. The horse ran from the scene when the employee appeared. The only significant marking on the reddish brown horse was a white star on his face. Where he came from remains a mystery.' "

Gil handed the paper back to Granddad. "I wonder what horse that could be. There aren't many around here, especially with a white marking like that."

"Are you sure it's not Rattler?" Granddad laid the paper in his lap.

"How could it be? There's no way he can open the gate now. At least I don't think so. I've kept it wired shut since he got out the first time." Gil ran his hands through his hair. "Come to think of it, though, I did find him outside the fence one day last week. I never did figure out how he had gotten out. Oh no, do you think it was Rattler?"

"Maybe not. It is curious, though, that a horse with a marking like Rattler's has been seen in town."

"It is kind of strange. He is rambunctious, but he's a spooker too. I don't think he'd be brave enough to go into town."

"You never know. He seems to be getting braver all the time." Granddad looked out the window. "I think I'd check that gate again just to make sure it is secure."

"I will, Granddad. I'd better hurry. Mom's probably got supper on the table. I'll see you tomorrow, Granddad. Bye, Grandma." Gil waved as he walked out the door.

The gate was just as Gil had left it. Ever since he'd been home from camp and even before then, he'd carefully wired the gate after latching it. There was no way Rattler could undo the wire. Gil gave it a tug. The only way Rattler could get out, he thought, is by jumping over the fence. But even if he did, he'd never be brave enough to go into town. Gil wondered about it all the way home.

The next day Gil and Billy spent the afternoon checking the fence for a place big enough for Rattler to get through. As they moved around the pasture, Rattler followed them. As they neared the creek, Rattler whinnied and shied away from it. They heard crackling in the underbrush. Gil and Billy stood still and listened. Rattler pranced nervously back and forth with flared nostrils. Suddenly, on the far side of the field beyond the creek, a big black bear appeared. He swung his head from side to side, sniffing the air.

"Wow, he's big!" Billy grabbed Gil's arm. "When you told me you saw a bear down here before, I didn't believe you. I thought you were making it up."

Gil pried Billy's fingers from his arm. "You can let go of my arm. He's not after us. He's probably looking for honey in that old tree over there. We've seen bees flying around that tree all summer. I bet he'll find quite a feast in there now."

As the bear moved toward the old tree, Rattler reared and snorted.

"From the looks of it, Rattler thinks that bear's after him." Billy pointed at Rattler. "He looks like he's about to . . ."

"Run!" Gil grabbed Billy and ran after Rattler. "We've got to see if he can get out. He'll lead us right to the place."

The boys ran as fast as they could. Rattler was way ahead of them, but they could see him heading straight for the gate.

"He can't get out there. What's he thinking?" Gil was breathing hard.

"He's not thinking. He's too scared. Maybe he's going to jump over it."

"He can't jump that gate. It's . . ." Gil watched in astonishment as Rattler soared over the gate and disappeared down the lane. "I started to say it's too high. But I guess he showed me. Now what do we do?"

"We stop and breathe for a while and then we get on our bikes and go after him." Billy hurried toward his bike. "Come on; we'll have to move to catch him."

Rattler was nowhere to be seen when the boys reached the end of the lane.

"Which way do you think he went?" Billy stopped his bike and looked both ways.

"His tracks are headed for town. We may be on the trail of the mystery horse that was in the paper yesterday." Gil put his foot on the pedal.

"The mystery horse?"

"I'll explain later. Just follow me and keep your eyes open."

Gil led the way to Charlie Snow's Diner first. The alley behind the diner was empty. No delivery boxes were stacked by the door. At least if the mystery horse is Rattler, he didn't return to the scene of the crime, Gil thought. He braked his bike behind the diner.

"What are we doing here?" Billy stopped beside him.

"We're looking for Rattler."

"At a diner?"

Gil laughed. "It does seem like a funny place for a horse to be, but the paper said that a mystery horse had been seen eating vegetables behind Charlie Snow's Diner. I thought if Rattler had come here once, he might come back. I guess either I was wrong, or Rattler isn't really the mystery horse."

"So what do we do now?"

"We think. Where else would a scared horse go?"

"You're asking me? I don't know how horses think." Billy lifted his ball cap and scratched his head. "What do you think?"

"I think we should just ride around for a while and see if we can find him. If he's really scared, there's no telling where he might go."

The boys rode down the alley and out on to Main Street. In front of the grocery store, a large crowd had gathered.

"Hey, what's going on at the Piggly-Wiggly?" Billy slowed down.

"I don't know. Let's go see."

As they neared the group, they could see that the people seemed to be in a ring around something in the parking lot. As they got closer, they could see that the something in the ring was a horse—Gil's horse. They squealed to a stop and let their bikes drop to the ground.

Gil pushed his way through the crowd. There stood Rattler, his halter firmly held by the manager of the store, Mr. Perkins. Gil stepped toward Rattler.

"You boys better stay back. This horse is pretty wild. He tried to break into my grocery store. There's no telling what damage he might've done or who he might've hurt if he'd gotten in there."

"Excuse me, sir, but I don't think he really wanted to go into your store. He was just scared and wasn't sure what to do."

Mr. Perkins stared at Gil. Rattler jerked his head up and down. Mr. Perkins let go of the halter as Gil grabbed it. Gil held out his hand with a sugar cube he pulled from his pocket.

"Does this horse belong to you, Gil?" Mr. Perkins wiped his forehead.

"Yes, sir, this is my horse, Rattler." Rattler took the sugar cube from Gil's hand. "I haven't had him long."

"And you're not going to keep him long if he keeps pulling stunts like these. He destroyed my display of apples on the front porch of the store. He ate a lot of them and trampled on the rest, almost four bushels of apples."

"I'm really sorry, Mr. Perkins. I'll pay for all of them."

"And will you also pay for the vegetables he ate from behind my diner?" Mr. Snow pushed through the crowd. "And the ones he bruised?"

"Sure I will." Gil held on to Rattler's halter. "I'll have to pay back a little at a time, though, 'cause I also have to pay for this horse. But if you'll send me a bill, I'll make good on it."

"Well, I guess the question now is how are you going to get him home?" Mr. Perkins stood with his hands on his hips. "I don't suppose you can ride him without a saddle."

"Actually, I could if I had a rope to use for reins." Gil rubbed Rattler's neck. "I've ridden him that way a few times in the pasture."

"But that's not the same as riding through town." Mr. Perkins looked concerned. "Are you sure you can handle him?"

"Yes, sir, if I have a rope."

"Well, I can get you some clothesline to use if that's all you need. I'll just add it to your bill."

"Thank you, Mr. Perkins."

Mr. Perkins disappeared into the store. When he returned, he handed Gil a package of clothesline. "I'll send you a bill. And you'd better make sure that horse doesn't get loose again."

Gil and Billy unwrapped the clothesline, cut off a piece, and tied it to the halter.

"What about your bike?" Billy asked. "How are you going to get it home?"

"Oh yeah, I forgot. How am I going to get it home?"

"Maybe you can leave it here and your mom can come pick it up for you." Billy stood up Gil's bike. "I'll go ask Mr. Perkins if that's all right."

"Thanks, Billy."

Gil waited for Billy to return. He felt kind of silly standing in a grocery store parking lot holding onto a horse. Why in the world did Rattler have to go and run away? And why did he have to run into town? Rattler nickered softly. "Sounds like an apology to me." He rubbed Rattler's soft nose. "I know you didn't mean to get into mischief, but how am I ever going to pay for all the stuff you messed up? I haven't even paid for you yet."

The next day Granddad again called Gil into the living room to see the newspaper. "You, Billy, and that rambunctious horse are quite famous."

Gil took the paper from Granddad. "I didn't know they took that picture. And that reporter didn't get any information from me." Gil read from the paper.

"Mystery horse is discovered at Piggly-Wiggly Market. The reddish brown horse with the white marking seen at Charlie Snow's Diner earlier this week was discovered at the Piggly-Wiggly Market, where he destroyed the apple display in front of the store. Mr. Perkins, the store manager, says the horse, named Rattler, belongs to Gil Freeman of Greendale. Mr. Freeman has agreed to pay all damages to Mr. Perkins and Mr. Snow. No formal charges have been filed."

Granddad took the paper from Gil when he was finished reading. "Sounds to me like that horse needs to earn his keep or at least enough to pay for the damages he caused."

"That would be great. But how? What can a horse do to earn money?"

Granddad looked down at the paper and then at Gil. "We'll have to think about that one. Remember, God has a solution to every problem."

Chapter 13

The next day, Granddad had Gil wheel him out to the family picnic area. "A breath of fresh air is good for a man. Especially after being cooped up for a while." He motioned for Gil to stop under an oak tree. "This'll do fine, Gil. Now you just sit right there at that picnic table, and we'll talk."

"What are we going to talk about, Granddad?" Gil sat on the picnic table with his feet on the bench.

"I think we need to solve that problem that developed this week. We need to figure out a way to let Rattler help you earn some money." Granddad looked out over the pasture. "It's time he learned to help."

"But what can he do?" Gil leaned forward with his elbows on his knees. "What can you do with a horse to earn money these days?"

"Now think about it, Gil. It'll come to you. What do most people want to do when they find out you have a horse?"

"They want to ride him."

"Exactly."

"Exactly what?"

"They want to ride him."

"I don't get it."

"If people want to ride your horse, how can you let them and still make some money?"

"Let them pay to ride Rattler." Gil hit his forehead with the heel of his hand. "Why didn't I think of that before?"

"I don't know; why didn't you?" Granddad looked very serious. Suddenly he began to laugh. "Maybe it's because you've been thinking only of things you can do for Rattler and not what he can do to help you."

"Do you think people would actually pay me to ride Rattler?"

"Maybe not grownups, but children will. Why don't you put out a sign and some fliers and see what happens?"

"What should I charge?"

"Let's start with a dollar for a ten-minute ride. How's that sound?"

By Monday afternoon, Gil had a hand-lettered sign ready to put at the end of the driveway. He and Billy rode their bikes around the neighborhood, handing out fliers with the times and the price for rides on Rattler. They planned to start giving rides on Saturday afternoon.

"Do you really think anyone will show up?" Billy wheeled his bike into the garage.

Gil hopped off his bike and kicked the kickstand into place. "Granddad thinks they will. I guess we'll have to wait and see."

"I'll be there to watch what happens." Billy pulled the garage door closed.

"You don't have to just watch; you can help too."

"Help do what? Direct the lines of millions of people who will come to ride your horse?"

"There's no need to be sarcastic." Gil tried unsuccessfully to grab Billy's cap. "If anybody comes, I'll need help lifting the little kids up onto Rattler's back. I won't be able to do that and hold the reins and keep him still. And we'll have to lead the horse around for all the little kids."

"I can do that." Billy grinned. "But don't expect me to work for nothing."

"How about some of Grandma's cooking?"

"I can't pass that up. I'll see you Saturday if I don't see you before."

"Yeah, see you."

Saturday was the perfect day for riding. The fliers Gil and Billy had handed out said that rides would be given between two and five in the afternoon. At 1:45 Gil had Rattler saddled and ready. Gil checked and rechecked the straps and buckles on the saddle and bridle.

"What's the matter, Gil? Do you think those straps have loosened since the last time you checked them?" Billy leaned on the gate.

"No, I just want to be sure everything is ready." Gil gave the saddle hitch one more tug. "I'd hate for some little kid to go sliding off onto the ground all of a sudden."

"Can't happen. You've checked everything so many times, the saddle can't possibly fall off." Billy grinned. He turned to look down the driveway toward the road. "No sign of anyone yet."

"Yet." Gil led Rattler around by the bridle. "They'll come."

And they did come. Soon Gil and Billy had a line of people waiting at the gate. Children of all sizes waited, money in hand. Billy took the money and deposited it in the cash box Granddad had loaned them, then he opened the gate to let in the next rider. While Gil held Rattler still, Billy lifted the rider up onto the horse or gave him a boost if he was older. After a while Gil and Billy switched places. Gil was delighted to see the money growing in the cash box. Granddad was right; this was a good way to earn money.

It was getting close to five when Gil told Billy there were only two riders left. He hadn't been paying much attention to all the faces that had passed by him, but when he turned around this time, he stopped still. There before him was a girl about his age. He couldn't help himself; he just stared.

"You are still giving rides, aren't you?" She smiled.

Gil nodded. His mouth felt dry.

"My little brother would like a ride." She held up the hand of the little boy beside her. "I do too, if that's all right."

Billy stopped at the gate behind Gil. "Hey Gil, help me out here. We're done with this ride."

Gil did not move. He just kept staring at the girl.

"Gil, are you deaf? I need some help."

The girl looked past Gil. "Don't you think you'd better help your friend?"

Suddenly Gil jerked awake. You'd think I'd never seen a girl before, he thought to himself. What a dope! He whirled around and flung open the gate. Without a word to Billy he reached up for the rider and lifted him down. "There you go, kid. Hope you had a good time."

He tried not to look at Billy.

"Hey Gil, who's the girl?" Billy ducked under Rattler's head to stand beside him. "Anybody you know?"

"Never seen her before in my life," Gil muttered under his breath. He opened the gate and stepped out. "Who wants to go first?" He looked at the little boy.

"Actually, I was hoping we could ride together." The girl stepped forward with her brother. "Danny likes to ride with me. But if you'd rather, he can go by himself. He has before where we used to live."

"I wouldn't mind your riding together, except my horse isn't used to that, and I'm not sure he'd like it. If you want, you can help me lead the horse while your brother rides, and then you can ride." Gil finally got up enough courage to look at the girl again.

"That would be great." The girl handed Gil two one-dollar bills.

Gil deposited the money in the box and opened the gate. "Billy, would you mind keeping an eye on the money while I take them around?"

"No problem." Billy looked from Gil to the girl and back again. "I can do that."

Gil lifted Danny up on Rattler's back. He took the bridle and stepped out to lead Rattler. The girl fell in step beside him.

"Do you think he'd let me lead him?" the girl asked after they had made one turn of the front pasture.

"I guess so. He's a little bit skittish around strangers. But he doesn't seem to mind you."

Gil stopped and handed the bridle to her. "By the way, my name's Gil. What's yours?"

"Julie Blakemore." Before Julie started walking, she reached into her pocket and pulled out a sugar cube. "Do you mind if I give him one?"

"Uh, no, but how'd you happen to have a sugar cube in your pocket?"

"My horse back home loves them. So when we decided to come over here today, I just stuck some in my pocket out of habit. I hoped you'd let me give him one."

"Sure, go ahead. He loves them."

Julie held out the sugar cube on her flat open hand. Rattler gently took the sugar cube from her. He shook his head up and down.

"That means he likes you. He does that only when he thinks everything is okay."

"Maybe it's just the sugar cube he likes, not me." Julie wiped her hand on her jeans. "You never know with horses."

Gil smiled. "You sure do know about horses. Where are you from?"

"Virginia. My dad got transferred to Greendale, and we weren't sure we would have a place to keep a horse, so I left it back home. My parents just bought the place up the road. There's a pasture and a small barn, but it needs a lot of work before we can keep a horse in it. So Princess is still in Virginia. That's why I came today. I'm homesick for my horse."

"I'm done," Danny called down from Rattler's back. "I want to get down."

"Oh, Danny, I'm sorry. How many times have we gone around?"

"Many times!" Danny bounced in the saddle.

"Hang on there, sport. I'll get you down. But let's get over by the gate." Gil took the bridle from Julie and led Rattler over to the gate. He lifted Danny down from Rattler's back. "There you go, Danny."

"What do you say, Danny?" Julie put her hand on Danny's head. "Say thank you."

"Thank you." Danny crossed his arms. "Thank you for the ride."

"Didn't you want to ride?" Gil turned to Julie.

"Oh, that's okay. I think we used up my ride on Danny. I had no idea we'd been out there so long. I am so sorry." She took Danny's hand. "I hope we didn't wear out your horse."

"I doubt it. But it looks like we wore out your brother." Gil pointed at Danny, whose head rested on Julie's hand.

"Mom won't mind. Maybe he'll be ready to go to bed tonight, for a change. Thanks again for letting me share your horse. Maybe I'll see you later."

"Come by anytime you get homesick for your horse, and you can ride Rattler. After all, I do owe you a ride."

Gil watched Julie walk down the driveway, her little brother in tow. When she turned and looked back, he waved.

Billy cleared his throat. "'Come by anytime you get homesick for your horse.' What's that supposed to mean?"

"Exactly what it sounds like. An invitation." Gil handed the money box to Billy. "Here, take this up to Granddad and tell him I'll be there in a little while."

"Shall I tell him why you've been out here so long? Because of a girl named Julie?" Billy grinned and ducked to escape Gil's playful swing.

"No, you don't need to say anything about Julie. She's just a girl."

"Just a girl who made you forget what time it was and how long poor Danny had been going in circles on that horse." Billy closed the gate between them as Gil came toward him. "Don't worry. You won't hear anymore about this from me. But just remember next Saturday that if Julie comes, she'd better be last in line—'cause if she's first, no one else will get a ride." Billy ran toward the house laughing.

Gil removed the saddle and bridle from Rattler and let him go to run free for a little while. By the time Gil had put everything away in the shed, Rattler was at the door ready to be groomed and fed.

With quick even strokes Gil brushed Rattler's coat. With each stroke an idea grew in his mind. By the time he was finished, he had a plan.

Chapter 14

"So this girl named Julie has a horse in Virginia, and you want to offer to let her bring her horse down here to stay with Rattler. Did I get that right?" Dad smiled at Gil across the table. "Are you sure this isn't just a plan to get to see Julie more?"

Gil could feel his face turning red. "No, Dad—well, sort of." Gil pushed his chair back from the table. "I just thought it would be nice for Rattler to have some company this fall when I go back to school. And I thought it would be nice for Julie to have her horse here instead of way up in Virginia. I know how I'd feel if Rattler were somewhere far away. So what do you think?"

"Do you know anything about this girl?" Mom asked.

"Not much. Just that her dad transferred here and they bought the Peterson place up the road. She's really nice, Mom. I'm sure you'd like her. But I'm not planning to marry her or anything. I just want to let her keep her horse in the shed with Rattler." Gil smiled at his mother. "She brought her little brother Danny with her for a ride, so that's a good sign she's a nice girl, isn't it?"

Gil's mother handed Gil the bowl of mashed potatoes for the third time. "That certainly sounds like a nice thing to do. Do they go to church anywhere?"

"I didn't get a chance to ask her, but they may not have had a chance to find a church yet. They haven't lived here long. I'll invite her—I mean them—next time I see her. What can I tell her about the horse?"

"We'll go out after supper and look over the place to make sure there'll be enough room. We'd better talk to Granddad about it too."

"I already asked him if it would be okay, and he said if it was okay with you, it was okay with him."

"You certainly have done some legwork on this already by getting the facts before you act."

"Just working my plan like you taught me, Dad." Gil took another big bite of potatoes.

After supper Gil and his dad drove over to Granddad's to look things over.

"Well, Gil, I'm not sure how Rattler will feel about sharing his living quarters with a total stranger, but it looks like there's plenty of room for both horses here and in the pasture." Gil's dad stood in the middle of the shed looking from side to side.

"Granddad thought there would be too. He said Rattler would be happier here this fall if he had another horse to be with since once school starts, I won't be around as much." Gil knocked a cobweb down from the corner of the doorway. "Besides, Julie really misses her horse, and this way she can come ride her as often as she wants to."

"And have you said anything to Julie yet?"

"No, sir. I thought I'd better make sure it was all right with you and Granddad first. Do you think it will be all right?"

"I think it will be fine, Son, as long as you and Julie understand that you are each responsible for your own horses."

"Oh, that's no problem, Dad. I'm sure Julie will agree."

"Tell you what. I'll give Mr. Blakemore a call and let him know that things are settled here, and you talk to Julie. Then they can figure out when they want to bring the horse down. Does that sound all right to you?"

"Sure thing, Dad. I'll talk to Julie."

About a week later a truck with a one-horse trailer pulled into the lane leading to Rattler's pasture. Julie and her dad got out of the truck. Gil and his dad were there to meet them.

"We can let Princess out into the pasture with Rattler to get acquainted while we unload the trailer," Gil said to Julie.

"While you kids do that, we'll go on up and visit with Granddad for a while. He always likes to make new friends." Gil's dad and Mr. Blakemore walked up to the house.

Julie unlatched the endgate of the trailer. "Easy, Princess, easy," she said.

"She likes being in a trailer about as much as Rattler does." Gil stepped back as Julie led a beautiful white mare out of the trailer. "Hope she doesn't mind sharing living quarters with Rattler."

"Oh, she won't mind. I don't think any horse likes being cooped up in a trailer, but as long as she has her own stall, she won't mind having another horse nearby. She's never been boarded by herself, so she's learned to get along." Julie rubbed Princess's soft nose. "See, she's calmed down already."

"Well, I guess we might as well go introduce her to Rattler." Gil opened the gate so Julie could put Princess in the pasture. Rattler was nowhere to be seen. "He must be over near the creek behind that big rock." He gave a sharp shrill whistle. Rattler appeared from behind the rock.

"Come on, Rattler; you've got company."

Rattler did not move. Princess pricked up her ears and listened.

"They'll be all right," Julie said. "It'll take them awhile to become friends."

Gil followed Julie around behind the trailer. "How much stuff do you have to unload, Julie?"

"Not much, just my grooming tools and my bridle and saddle." She pointed to a shelf in the trailer.

Gil gave a low whistle. "That's some saddle. Where'd you get it?" He lifted the saddle from the shelf and carried it into the shed. He ran his finger over the silver inlay and along the silver edges. "This sure outclasses Rattler's."

"A man in Texas gave that saddle to my dad after my dad did some work for him. Dad gave it to me when he realized how serious I was about showing horses. It seems to suit Princess."

"That's for sure. This saddle looks like it belongs to royalty. I'll put it up here on the shelf next to Rattler's two saddles. I don't think we'll have any trouble telling them apart." Gil put the saddle on the shelf. "It makes those other two saddles look shabby."

"Oh, I don't think so." Julie stepped back to look. "They're just a different sort of saddle, sort of rustic looking."

"That makes me feel better." Gil laughed. "I wonder if Princess is making Rattler feel rustic too." He led the way around the truck. "I wonder how they're doing?"

"Looks like they're doing just fine." Julie pointed to the middle of the pasture. "Rattler is acting like a true gentleman."

"I'm surprised." Gil watched the two horses together. "I was afraid Rattler would feel like he had to defend his territory. I thought he might nip and bite, but it looks like they're good friends already. I do believe he's found a friend."

"It looks that way," Julie said.

Rattler led Princess over the pasture from the creek to the rock and around the fence. In the late afternoon sun, the two horses appeared at times to be one horse as they walked side by side.

"No jealousy there," Gil said. "I don't think we have to worry about a thing."

Suddenly, Gil and Julie spotted a hot-air balloon rising over the tops of the trees beyond the lower pasture.

"They're flying really low. I wonder if they're in trouble." Gil pointed. "They look like they're having trouble staying above the trees." He ran toward the house. "I'd better tell Dad and Granddad."

"I'll go with you."

"No, you stay here and keep an eye on the horses. Rattler's a spooker, and there's no telling what he might do if that balloon comes down here."

Gil returned just as the balloon came to rest at the lower end of the pasture.

"Where's Rattler?" Gil scanned the pasture for the horse.

Julie pointed toward the shed. "Over there."

In the shadow of the shed stood Rattler and Princess. Rattler stood between Princess and the balloon as if to protect her.

"I can't believe he didn't get spooked." Gil opened the gate and held it for Julie.

"I think he was really afraid and wanted to run," Julie said. "But because Princess was there, he thought he needed to protect her. Maybe his instinct to protect was greater than his fear."

"He's just getting braver all the time." Gil wired the gate shut behind them. "We'd better see what we can do to help that balloon crew."

As they ran toward the balloon, they could see three people in the basket. Two of them jumped out and grabbed the ropes as the balloon deflated. Gil looked back to see how Rattler was handling the noise. Rattler was standing his ground between Princess and the balloon. His ears and muscles were twitching, but that was all.

"Sorry we had to come down in your pasture. Hope we didn't scare your horses too much." The third man climbed out of the basket. He wiped his hands on his pants and held a hand out to Gil. "Name's Mark. Mark Collins. These are my fellow balloonists, Jack and Pete."

Gil shook the man's hand. "When we first saw you coming down, we thought you were going to crash. It looked like you were having trouble staying above the trees."

"Well, I can't say we weren't getting a little worried there." Mark pushed back his hair. "We got blown off course, so we were looking for a clear place to land. Your pasture was the first place big enough. But we didn't anticipate having to come in so close to the trees. It was a little tricky."

"How did you keep from hitting the trees?"

"We regulate the amount of hot air in the balloon to go up or down. When we want it to go up, we give another blast of hot air. When we want to come down, we open the flap at the top of the balloon to let out some hot air. We use the flap at the top to deflate the balloon too. We just open the flap and let all the air out a little at a time. If we had time, I'd take you up and show you, but it's going to be dark before too long. By the way, what are your names?"

"My name's Gil, and this is Julie."

"Nice to meet you, Gil and Julie. Are those your horses?"

"Yes, sir. The mare is Julie's, and the quarter horse is mine. He's usually a spooker, but he's doing okay right now."

"Looks like he's got his mind on protecting that pretty mare instead of on himself. Protecting a woman usually brings out the strength in a man. That's how God intended it."

Gil tried not to look surprised. "Are you a Christian?"

"We all are. I know we look a bit scruffy right now. But we clean up real nice on Sundays. Don't we, guys?"

"Sure we do." The other two men came over to join them. "Are you kids Christians too?"

"I am," Gil said.

"I am too," Julie added.

Gil looked over at her and smiled. Mom will be happy to hear that, he thought.

"You just never know where you're going to find fellow Christians, do you? Sometimes they drop right out of the blue almost on your heads." Mark laughed. "Tell you what. We always have a word of prayer when we land to thank the Lord for keeping us safe. Would you like to join us? Then we'll figure out how to get this balloon and all of us back to where we came from."

They bowed their heads, and each one of the men said a brief sentence or two, thanking God for their safety and for the beauty of all they had seen. When they had finished, Mark clapped Gil on the back.

"You'll have to come ballooning with us sometime, you and Julie here. We always like to give a ride or two to those who help us out."

"I'd like that." Gil looked at the large folded balloon. "Where are you from, anyway?"

"Just the other side of Pine City." Jack laughed. "You thought we'd come a lot farther than nineteen miles, didn't you? The truth is, we belong to a local balloon club. In a few weeks there is going to be a fly-in, so we thought we'd better check out our balloon. We got off course and lost our ground crew, and now here we are. Not a very exciting story, is it?"

"I think it is," Julie said.

"I do too," Gil added. "I guess my question is, how are you going to get back? Is your ground crew going to pick you up?"

"Therein lies the problem." Pete pushed the other two men aside and stepped between them. "We lost radio contact with them an hour ago, so we think they gave up on us and went home. So I guess we'll just have to walk, carrying our trusty balloon and basket on our backs."

Jack pointed to the horses. "We could borrow them."

"I don't think Rattler and Princess could hold all of you and the balloon too." Gil looked from the men to the horses.

"I was just kidding, kid. I wouldn't burden those gorgeous horses with the likes of us." Jack lifted his hat and pushed back his hair. "I guess we'll just have to hoof it ourselves. Excuse the expression."

"But you can't carry that balloon and basket, can you?"

"No, I was kidding about that too."

"We'll help you out." Gil's dad spoke from behind Gil. "I'm Walt Freeman, Gil's dad. The three of us, Gil's grandfather, Julie's dad, and I, watched you from the window of the house. I'll be glad to give you a ride wherever you need to go. There's an old pickup my dad keeps around here to help with hauling hay, and it will get you there and get us back as long as it's not too far. I think we can even fit your balloon and basket in the back."

"We thank you, Mr. Freeman. We were trusting the Lord to put us down in a safe place. And He did."

"He does provide for us, doesn't He?" Gil's dad led the way to the truck.

Chapter 15

"You're kidding, right?" Billy lay back in the grass with his hands under his head. "You want me to get up at midnight to come over here and stare up at the sky in hopes of seeing a shooting star?"

Gil, Billy, and Julie sat on the grass near one of the picnic tables. They had spent the morning mucking out the stalls in the shed. Gil and Julie had told Billy he didn't have to help, but Billy had insisted. Now the three were recovering from the smelly, messy job.

Gil threw a small stick at Billy's foot. "No, I'm not kidding. And it's not just a chance you'll see a shooting star. If the sky is clear, you will for sure."

"How do you know that? Is there some kind of guarantee?" Billy rolled up on his side to look at Gil.

"He knows that this is the time of year for meteor showers, and next Friday and Saturday are the best times to see the shooting stars." Julie looked at Gil. "Isn't that what your grandfather told me?"

"Yes, he said that August 11 and 12 are the best days to see them. But the best time to see them is between midnight and 2:00 A.M. in the northeast sky. Our family has been watching them for as long as I can remember. It's one of our family traditions. This year Dad said we could invite some friends to come with us." Gil threw another stick at Billy. "So do you want to come or not, Billy?"

"What about Julie? Aren't you going to invite her?" Billy threw the stick back.

"Dad already invited her whole family to join us. So what are you going to do, sleep or watch stars?"

"I don't know. I'll have to think about it. I don't give up my sleep for much, and I'm not sure this will be worth it."

"Trust me, Billy; you don't want to miss it. Dad borrowed a high-powered telescope this year, so we can see the planet Jupiter in the eastern sky."

At midnight the next Friday, Dad pulled the station wagon into the driveway at Granddad's house. "Now you guys be quiet," he said to Gil and Billy, "at least until we get out in the pasture. We don't want to wake everybody up at this time of night."

"What about Julie and her family? Are we going to wait for them?" Gil peered out the back window.

"We'll give them a few more minutes. They should be here any minute."

The stillness of the night surrounded the car as they sat quietly waiting. Then the bright headlights of a car swung across the windows.

"There they are," Billy said. He opened his door and slid out. Gil slid out behind him.

"It doesn't look like the whole family." Gil closed the door as quietly as he could.

"How can you tell?" Billy rubbed his eyes. "Those headlights blinded me, and now I can't see a thing."

"Your eyes will readjust in a minute." Gil's dad lifted the telescope out of the back of the car. "You're right, Gil; it's not the whole family. Mrs. Blakemore stayed home with the younger children. Just Julie and her dad came. Here they come now."

The horses followed them down into the lower pasture. Rattler nuzzled the bag of popcorn Gil carried.

"No, boy, this isn't for you. You'll have to wait 'til I can get my hand free to give you a sugar cube."

Rattler nuzzled Gil's hand again. Princess was doing the same thing to Julie.

"Looks like they're glad to see us," Julie said.

Her dad laughed. "It looks more like those two horses want a midnight snack." He shifted the small cooler of pop to his other hand. "They think that's why we came."

"They'll have to be satisfied with a sugar cube when we get a chance to give it to them."

When the group reached the lower corner of the pasture, they looked toward the northeast sky.

"There's one!"

"Where? I missed it."

"There goes another one!"

The shooting stars began to come every few minutes. The sky looked like a slow-motion fireworks display. But there was no sound from them. Just the sound of Rattler's occasional neighing.

"You know those aren't really stars, don't you?" Billy rubbed his neck as he tilted his head back farther.

"What are they, then?" Gil knew, but he wanted to see if Billy did.

Billy stood up and cleared his throat. "Shooting stars are actually meteor showers. Meteor showers happen when the earth crosses the dust-filled orbit of a comet. When pieces of dust or debris, called meteoroids, enter the earth's atmosphere, they heat up and glow, producing meteors, or 'shooting stars.' Fragments that hit the earth are called meteorites." Billy sat back down on the ground beside Gil.

"Wow, Billy. You know more about this than I thought you did." Gil looked over at his friend. "I thought you didn't even know what I was talking about."

"I didn't. But I went home and looked it up in the encyclopedia. I didn't know stars could be so interesting. I also know that in August around the constellation Perseus, when the meteors or shooting stars are most plenteous, they are called Perseids." Billy threw his shoulders back and stuck out his chest. "How's that for learning something?"

Gil laughed. "You even sound like an encyclopedia. You are some kind of guy, you know that?" He held out his hand for Billy to shake.

"Thanks." He shook Gil's hand. "I thought I'd better know something."

"You know more than I do, that's for sure." Julie smiled at Billy.

"Oh, it's nothing."

Gil's dad put his arm around Billy's shoulders. "It's great any time you learn something, especially on your own initiative."

Gil grinned at Billy. "See, you even made points with my dad."

"What is the possibility that one of the bigger meteorites could hit the earth?" Julie stared up at the sky. "Could that really happen?"

"Yes. Occasionally a small meteorite does hit the earth, but the ones we're looking at now are many miles away. Most of them burn up before they reach the earth." Gil stood beside her. "I don't think we have to worry about one falling on our heads."

"What we do need to worry about is being able to get up in the morning." Julie's dad picked up the empty popcorn bag. "Everyone looked at the planets through the telescope, and we're officially out of food, so we can go home."

"That's probably not a bad idea," Gil's dad said. "Even though tomorrow's Saturday, we do have work to do."

"It looks like most of the show's over, anyway." Gil gathered up the empty pop cans. "Time to head for home."

"Gil, look! What is that?" Julie pointed at an animal crossing the pasture just ahead of them.

"It's probably a skunk or a raccoon. I don't see any white stripe, but it's hard to see even with the moonlight."

"There's one sure way to find out which it is," Billy said. "All we have to do is get too close, and if it's a skunk, he'll lift his tail and let us have it. No escape from that smell!"

Mr. Blakemore laughed. "And no getting rid of it afterwards, either."

They stopped talking and crept a little closer. The animal saw them and disappeared into the underbrush along the creek.

"I'm pretty sure it was a raccoon," Gil's dad said. "Did you see its eyes? A raccoon's eyes shine in the dark. I heard once that if the eyes shine orange, it's a she coon. And if the eyes shine green, it's a he coon. That's what I heard, anyway."

"Granddad says that raccoons come out at night," Gil said. "That's when they hunt for food."

Julie caught up with Gil. "Aren't they the animals that wash their food before eating it?"

"That's what people say. Granddad says they don't really wash it. They just dunk it in the water before they eat it. A lot of their food, like crayfish, comes from the water, but they dunk that too." Gil laughed. "I guess they just like their food wet. It would be fun to watch them to see what they do."

"Maybe that can be another midnight project for us, Gil—raccoon watching," Dad said. "But right now I'm ready to go home."

By the time the group reached the cars, the last of the shooting stars had disappeared from the sky. Somewhere in the distance a dove gave its mournful call.

"That is the saddest sounding bird I've ever heard, I think," Gil's dad said.

"Isn't that a mourning dove?" Gil asked.

"Yes, it is. They say it gets its name partly because it makes such a sad sound. It sounds almost like someone sobbing with grief."

"It is a sad sound," Julie said when they heard it again. "Oh, I don't want this adventure to end on a sad note."

"Well, we can't stop the bird's mournful note, but we can praise God for all His wonderful creation. Why don't we take a minute to thank Him for all we saw and enjoyed tonight?" Gil's dad looked at Gil. "Would you like to pray for all of us, Son?"

"Sure, Dad."

After Gil prayed and thanked God for all they had seen, everyone said a quick good night, or rather good morning. Gil and Billy climbed into the back seat of the station wagon.

"You know, Gil, things sure looked different to me tonight than they would have a few weeks ago. Being saved sure makes a difference in how you look at things."

"It sure does, Billy. It sure does."

Chapter 16

With school just a couple of weeks away, Gil spent as much time as he could with Rattler. He loved to ride Rattler around the pasture. And recently he had even been able to ride Rattler out along the road and on the trails through the nearby woods. Sometimes Julie and Princess would join them. If they went somewhere a bike could go, Billy would come along too.

On this particular afternoon, Julie and Gil followed a trail through the woods, not knowing where it would take them. They knew it headed in the general direction of town, but they did not know where it would come out. When they finally reached the end of the trail, they discovered that they were near the side road that led to town. There was a small turnout nearby with a picnic table.

"Looks like we followed the right trail this time." Julie slid off Princess's back. "This is a good place to eat the lunch my mom packed for us."

"You didn't tell me she packed us a lunch." Gil dismounted and tied Rattler's reins to a low-hanging branch. "You've been holding out on me." He grinned.

"Some things are better kept a secret until the appropriate time. If I had told you my mom had packed a lunch, you would've wanted to eat it then and there. I know you. You're always hungry."

"Right now I'm starved. When do we eat?"

"Just let me get Princess tied up, and I'll unpack the lunch."

Just then Rattler gave a loud whinny. He was looking away from them in the direction of town.

"What is it, boy? What do you see?" Gil tried to follow Rattler's eyes. "I sure don't see anything."

"Maybe he doesn't see it, but he just smells something," Julie said. "Whatever it is, Princess senses it too. Look at her."

Both Rattler and Princess had their ears pricked up, their noses lifted to sniff the breeze.

"I still don't see anything." Gil turned back to the picnic table. "It can't be too bad or Rattler would be going crazy. Let's eat."

Suddenly, Rattler reared and whinnied. He pulled against the reins.

"Easy, boy, it's just—" Gil turned to look "—an elephant!" Gil and Julie shouted the words at the same time.

Rattler stood still with Gil's hand on the halter. But his sides heaved and his muscles quivered.

Gil patted Rattler's side. "I don't blame you for being scared, Rattler. I'd be scared too if I'd never seen an elephant before. I'm not scared, just confused. Where do you think he came from?"

"I have no idea. But I can tell you who doesn't care at all that there's an elephant walking down the road." Julie reached for Princess's halter. "Princess isn't even interested."

Princess had found a small clump of grass on the edge of the turnout and was eating it.

Gil turned Rattler's head toward Princess. "Look how calm Princess is. Why can't you be like that? But then I guess I shouldn't expect you to be anything but what you are."

The elephant passed slowly in front of them. It did not even turn to look at them.

"I can't believe this. There's an elephant walking down the road, and no one seems to care. I wonder who he belongs to?"

"He belongs to the circus." A small man with a stick in his hand paused a moment to get his breath. "But I'm responsible for him and, trust me, I do care that he is walking down this road in what, I might add, is quite the wrong direction."

Gil looked at the elephant. "An elephant from the circus, of course. But how did he get away?"

"We walk the elephants from the railroad station to the fairgrounds because that is the only way to get them there. Once we get them off the train, there is no truck big enough to carry them. It does them good to get exercise after being on the train." The man wiped the sweat from his forehead. "Zimbala decided he did not like the way we were going and turned the other way. I've been trying to get him to go the other direction all morning. Every time I get him going in the right direction, he turns around again. He is getting tired now, though."

The elephant had stopped just beyond where they stood. He swayed his trunk from side to side and then suddenly trumpeted. Rattler reared, knocking Gil to the ground. Princess pranced wildly.

"Easy, girl. It's okay. Steady." Julie held tightly to the halter. "Gil, are you all right?"

Gil accepted a hand from the elephant trainer and stood up. Rattler had backed as far away from the elephant as he could get.

"It's a good thing I tied those reins around that branch and didn't just loop them. Rattler'd be half way to Georgia by now if I hadn't."

"I am sorry my elephant scared your horses. He must smell water."

"There's a creek at the bottom of that gully." Gil pointed in that direction. "That must be what he smells."

"Do you think he'll trumpet again?" Julie patted the panting horse beside her.

"I do not think so. I hope he does not try to get down to that water." The man sat down on the bench of the picnic table. "For now he is not going anywhere. Maybe the others will come soon to help me."

"What others?"

"Other trainers. When they see that Zimbala and I are gone, they will come for us."

"But how will they know where you are?" Julie asked.

"This was the only way we could have gone. All other roads are crowded with people. They will figure it out. They had to get the others to the fairgrounds and stake them there before we lost them all."

"Does this happen often?" Julie looked from the trainer to the elephant.

"No, not usually. It's just that Zimbala has a mind of his own. We have trained him just like the others, but he likes to wander, and we cannot seem to convince him not to."

Just then a truck came around the curve in the road. It was moving slowly.

"Help has come." The man stood and waved his hands. "We are here!"

Several men jumped from the back of the truck. Some had short sticks and one man had a long one with a hook on the end. After a quick command and a few prods with the sticks, the elephant dropped to his knees. The man with the hook scrambled up onto the elephant and sat behind his big ears. He said just one word: "Up." The elephant stood to his feet. A few more quick commands and the elephant turned in the right direction.

"The master has spoken. Zimbala will not wander now. Someday I will be a master trainer."

With a quick bow, the man joined his friends in the truck. The truck turned around and followed the lumbering elephant and his rider.

"No one's going to believe this story, that's for sure." Gil sat down on the bench with a thud. "I'm not sure I believe it myself."

"Well, if you don't believe it, all you have to do is remember how Rattler was acting and you'll know something strange happened." Julie sat down across the table. "But an elephant? Who would have thought?"

Later that evening, Gil told his dad about the elephant.

"I'm telling you, Dad, there was an elephant in the road." Gil followed his dad into the family room. "Julie and I were at that little picnic area on Old Highway 24 and around the curve in the road came an elephant! Scared poor Rattler to death."

"And you say he came from the circus?" Dad settled into his recliner. "I didn't even know the circus was in town."

"I saw the posters at the grocery store the other day, but I didn't notice the date. But the man told us that the elephant was from the circus. And since we don't have a zoo, I can't think of any other place he might have come from, can you?"

"No, but I still can't believe you saw an elephant on Old Highway 24. What a story!"

Dad unfolded the evening paper. Gil looked over his shoulder. There on the front page of the paper was a picture of Zimbala walking through town with a man on his back.

"That's them!" Gil pointed at the picture. "I know Billy won't believe me when I tell him, but now I have proof."

"You sure do, Son." Dad lowered the paper. "By the way, Granddad called my office right before I left to tell me that he's seen a couple of kids hanging around the pasture the last couple of days. They seem to show up just about the time you leave. He says he hasn't seen them do anything wrong yet, but he thought you might keep an eye out for them. He also thought you might want to check and make extra sure everything is secure."

"Maybe I'd better ride over there right now. It's not dark yet, and if they're hanging around maybe I can talk to them and find out what they want." Gil reached for his ball cap.

"Just be sure to give yourself enough time to get home before dark and in time for supper. Whatever your mother's cooking sure smells good."

"Yes, sir. You know me. I never miss a meal."

Chapter 17

When Gil arrived at his grandfather's house, the sheriff's car stood in the driveway. Gil parked his bike in its usual spot. Without bothering to knock on the back door, he rushed in.

"Granddad, you all right?" he called as he ran through the kitchen.

"I'm fine, Gil. There's nothing the matter with me."

Gil skidded to a stop in the doorway to the living room. Granddad was in his usual place by the window. Standing beside him was Sheriff Keener and seated on the couch were two boys about Gil's age.

"Come on in, Son," the sheriff said. "We were just about to get the whole story out of these two young men."

"The whole story about what?" Gil looked at his grandfather.

"Sit down, Gil, and I'll start at the beginning."

Gil sat down in the first available chair, a little hard wooden one that stood just inside the door. He pulled it forward so he could see everyone in the room. "Go ahead, Granddad; I'm listening." He looked at the two boys on the couch. They tried to look tough, but finally looked away.

"Your dad probably told you that I called about a couple of kids hanging around the pasture," Granddad said.

"That's why I'm here. I thought I'd better check over here this evening to make sure everything's all right. It looks like it was a good thing I did." Gil glared at the boys on the couch.

"Well, not long after I called your dad, I looked out the window and saw these two boys sneaking around the shed. Rattler and Princess were down toward the creek, so I figured they couldn't bother them. But I knew there was a lot of stuff they could steal if they had a mind to."

Granddad looked from the boys to the sheriff. "I called Sheriff Keener right then because I wasn't sure what they were up to, and they looked mighty suspicious. While I waited, I picked up my binoculars and just watched to see what would happen."

"I didn't see the boys for some time, and then they appeared on the other side of the shed. They headed down toward the creek. They spooked the horses and chased them in opposite directions. Princess ran down toward the creek trying to get away from them. They cornered her there and started throwing mud balls at her. Rattler must have sensed she was in danger because he came charging over from the rock and reared up and pawed the air near the boys. They had enough sense to run. And they ran straight into Sheriff Keener. They were just getting ready to tell their side of the story when you came in." Granddad looked at the boys. "Go ahead. We're listening. Tell Gil your names before you start, though."

Both boys crossed their arms and slumped back against the couch.

"You'd better sit up and do some fast talking. You're in enough trouble as it is. You don't want to get into any more trouble by not talking, do you?"

One of the boys sat up and uncrossed his arms. "We didn't do nothin'. We were just having a little fun."

"What's your name, Son?" Granddad asked.

"Brad."

"Well, Brad, what is it that you didn't do? You were down around and in that shed an awfully long time to be doing nothing."

"Don't say nothin', Brad. You don't have to. My dad says so. They can't make you say what you don't want to say." The other boy pulled Brad back on the couch. "Just keep your mouth shut, and they can't do nothin' to you. It's the old man's word against ours."

"I'm afraid, in this case, that's not necessarily so. Mr. Freeman saw you throw mud balls at the horses, and he saw you in and around the shed. He may not know what you did in the shed, but he saw you there. Because no one else has been there since, anything that is wrong inside that shed is your doing. Now do you want to tell us what you did, or do you want me to take you down to my office and hold you 'til your parents come?"

Brad scooted up to the edge of the couch. "We didn't do much in the shed. Just messed it up a little. We were just going to look around, but Nate said we should have some fun. He threw the saddles and stuff on the floor."

"You helped me."

"And then he told me to throw manure on them. He wanted to set the shed on fire and make it look like we'd rescued the horses. He said we'd be heroes, and everyone would make a big deal about it."

"Would you just shut your mouth, Brad? You're messing everything up. Nobody would be the wiser if you'd kept your mouth shut." Nate grabbed Brad's arm and tried to pull him back.

Brad jerked away. "At first it was fun, messing up the shed. But when Nate started talking about setting it on fire, I got scared."

"What happened then?" Gil leaned forward in his chair.

"I ran outside and Nate came after me. He was still trying to talk me into setting the shed on fire. Then he saw the horses. He told me to run at them and scare them. He said he just wanted to see what they would do."

"And do you always do what Nate tells you to do?" Sheriff Keener asked.

"Most of the time."

"Even when it's wrong?"

Nate leaned forward. "We were just having fun."

"You may have thought it was fun. But the horses certainly weren't having any fun." Gil stared at Nate.

"Well, that big horse almost killed us. He would have too if we hadn't gotten out of there. Maybe I should tell my dad to sue you for keeping such a dangerous animal around." Nate scowled back at Gil. "How would you like that?"

"Rattler is not a dangerous animal. He's never hurt anyone." Gil stood up. "It sounds like he was just protecting Princess from the two of you."

"Sit down, Gil." Granddad pointed to the chair. "There's no need to get angry. These boys are wrong and they know it. It just seems a little harder for Nate to admit it."

"Why did you throw mud balls at the horses, anyway?" Gil sat down on the edge of the chair.

" 'Cause we wanted to. Is that a good enough reason for you?"

"No!"

"Gil." Granddad's voice was stern.

Gil slid back in the chair. "I'm sorry, Granddad. It's just that it makes me so mad that these kids were out there tormenting Rattler and Princess. Rattler must have sensed danger, or he wouldn't have gone to Princess's defense."

"I know, Gil. But getting angry isn't going to help. Remember, before you act, get all the facts. Sheriff Keener, I think you and Gil need to take a walk down to the shed with these boys and see what damage they did there. We already know what they did to the horses because I saw them do it. After you've seen the damage, we'll call their parents and work out a suitable punishment."

"You're not going to press charges?" Sheriff Keener sounded surprised.

"No, I don't think that's what these boys need. They need a good dose of hard work to channel their excess energy and occupy their time. It seems as though they have too much of it and too little common sense, or they wouldn't be going around making mischief."

The shed was worse than Gil had imagined. Not only had the boys thrown everything on the floor and covered it with manure, but they had also smeared the walls of the shed inside and out. There did not appear to be any permanent damage, just a lot of cleaning up to do.

Sheriff Keener described the shed to Granddad when they returned to the house. "That's about the size of it, Mr. Freeman. Nothing was destroyed, just messed up. A good scrubbing, repainting, and shoveling ought to set things right."

"I appreciate that, Sheriff. Now if you'll call the boys' parents and ask them to come on over here, we'll talk about what these boys can do to set the record straight."

Gil wanted to stay and hear the end of it, but Granddad insisted that he go on home.

"There's no need for you to stay. You can't do any more to fix things. It's my shed and I'll see that it gets put back right." Granddad wheeled his chair into the kitchen behind Gil. "You just go on home and tell your folks about these two and ask them to pray that God will get ahold of their hearts. What they need is to be saved. But God's going to have to soften their hard hearts first. What a shame to be so young and already so hard. You go on now and pray for them too."

"All right, Granddad. But I want to know what happens."

"Don't you worry about that, Gil my boy. You'll get the lowdown because you're the one who's going to be supervising the work crew." Granddad smiled. "Don't you worry about a thing. God let these boys come our way so we could help them, and we'll do our best to do just that."

The next morning Gil was on the backdoor step half an hour earlier than usual. He thought Granddad would've called him last night, but he hadn't. Gil raised his hand to knock since it was early, but before he could hit the door, it opened.

"Come on in, Gil. We've been expecting you." Grandma held the door open and let him pass. "Sit right down there at the table, and I'll get you some sausage and eggs just as soon as the eggs are ready. Granddad should be here in a minute."

Gil went around to his usual chair and sat down to wait for Granddad. The smell of sausage made his stomach growl. Sausage and eggs was worth getting up early for, anyway.

Granddad wheeled his chair into the kitchen and right up to the table. "Good morning, Gil. Did you sleep well?"

Gil stared across the table at his grandfather. How could he sleep well when he'd been waiting all night to find out what happened? But he couldn't very well say that to Granddad. "I slept okay, I guess. I was sort of wondering what happened after I left here yesterday."

"I'm sure you have been. And just as soon as we get our breakfast on the table and have a word of prayer, I'll tell you."

Grandma set a plate in front of Gil and another in front of Granddad. "You fellas go ahead. I'm right in the middle of making a cake for the bake sale over at the school, so I'm going to eat while I work. Walt, I'll stand right here while you ask the blessing."

Gil could hardly wait for Granddad to say amen. He tried to listen to what he was saying, but all he could think about was those kids and their punishment. Finally, Granddad said amen and picked up his fork.

"I guess you want to know what happened, don't you?" Granddad took a bite of sausage and chewed it carefully. "But before I tell you, let me tell you why I didn't call you last night and fill you in."

Gil laid his fork down. "I am kind of curious about that."

"I didn't call you last night because I thought you needed a night to get over your anger at those boys. I knew you were real mad at them for what they did to those horses, and I thought if you had some time to get over that you might feel more kindly toward them. They really are just a couple of rowdy kids with too much energy and time, and they end up getting into mischief. They're just rambunctious."

"I know they are, Granddad. I'd probably be the same way if I had too much time to spend looking for something to do."

"You certainly don't have that problem, do you?"

Gil laughed. "Not right now, anyway."

"Now you go on and eat while I tell you what happened. I think you'll agree that we came up with a pretty good plan."

Granddad explained that the boys were going to come back and clean the shed inside and out and repaint it. They were also going to come back once a week to help Gil care for the horses.

"They're going to help me take care of Rattler and Princess?" Gil didn't mean to bang his fork against the plate. "After what they did to them?"

"How else will they learn the proper way to treat them if somebody doesn't teach them?"

"But does the teacher have to be me?"

"Who else would you suggest? You're the best one I know. You know the ropes and you also know the Lord. They need to learn about both of those, don't you think?"

"I'm sure they do, but I don't think they are interested in learning about either one."

"I think you'll be surprised. Brad has already shown signs of wanting to learn, and Nate, I discovered, is simply a product of his father's way of thinking."

"What do you mean by that?" Gil finished the last swallow of milk in his glass.

"When his father came last night, and the sheriff filled him in on what had happened, the man pulled out his billfold and offered to pay for the damages. When I suggested that his son would profit more by having to work off his debt, he became very angry and said that was unfair treatment. He did not think his son should have to do anything. It's no wonder the boy is the way he is if he's never had to take responsibility for his own actions."

"How did you get his father to agree to the punishment?"

"Sheriff Keener just told him that it was my way or I would press formal charges against the boys for vandalism. I guess he liked the first plan better because he finally agreed. Brad's father was a little more agreeable from the very beginning. That's why I think you can have a great influence over these boys. They've stopped listening to adults because they've been getting mixed messages. They need to see someone closer to their own age doing right and working hard. Maybe then they'll be open to hearing the truth of the gospel."

"I'll do my best, Granddad. But I'm not sure I'm going to like it."

Chapter 18

It would take two full days of hard work to get the shed cleaned up and another day to paint it, Gil decided. The mess on the inside wasn't so bad, but the sun had baked the manure and straw on the outside until it was like brick mortar. He started the boys to work on the outside while he rescued the saddles from the mess on the floor.

"I don't know why we have to do this, anyway," Nate said to Brad for the hundredth time.

"Because we're the ones who put it there in the first place. If you hadn't had the bright idea of smearing this place up, we wouldn't be here." Brad scraped at the manure with a putty knife.

"I haven't heard you complaining. I think you like this stuff."

Brad stopped working and faced his friend. "I don't like this stuff, as you call it, but I do like Gil. There aren't many guys who'd do what he's doing and not take it out on us at the same time. He's a good guy."

Nate sat down on the nearest bale of hay. "He just acts that way 'cause he knows his granddad's up there in the house with binoculars trained on him all the time. If good old Granddad weren't watching, he'd be all over us."

"That's where you're wrong, Nate." Gil, who had heard the entire conversation, stepped out of the shed.

"See, Brad, he's spying on us. Trying to catch us messing up so he can tell the sheriff."

"I wasn't spying. Next time you decide to talk about me, you'd better check to make sure I'm out of earshot. This shed wasn't made to be soundproof, you know." Gil looked at the wall where Brad was working. "That looks good, Brad. You keep working like that and we'll be done sooner than we thought."

"Got any good words for me, preacher boy?" Nate crossed his arms and glared at Gil.

"If you were doing some good work, I'd have some good words. But since, from the looks of it, you haven't done much of anything, I'm afraid I don't have much to say."

"It's a good thing Granddad can't hear you. He might not think you were being nice enough or Christian enough."

"Now that you mention it, maybe I should tell you that Granddad can hear most of what we say out here. He has excellent hearing, and sound carries from here to there real well. As far as what you said to Brad about my doing what I do because he's watching, I do what I do because God is watching, not Granddad. God's the One that I want to please. And by pleasing God, I'll also please my grandfather, who is one of the people who taught me to love and serve God."

"There you go preaching again." Nate leaned back on the bale of hay and closed his eyes. "Wake me up when the sermon's over."

"The sermon won't ever be over, Nate. What I believe is what I live by and a part of everything I do. Now I think you'd better get up and do your share of this work because, as I remember it, most of this was your idea." Gil headed back into the shed. "By the way, when we get the shed clean and painted, we'll spend the night down here one night. You know, camp out under the stars. It'll be great."

Nate rolled his eyes. "Can't wait." He slid off the bale of hay and went back to work.

Gil glanced up at the house as he went back into the shed. He was glad Granddad and Grandma were up there praying. He needed it. Nate was a lot tougher than Granddad said he'd be.

By the end of the third day, the shed looked clean and fresh with its new coat of paint. After supper on the final day, Gil, Nate, and Brad unrolled their sleeping bags on the straw they had spread beside the shed.

Gil laughed as Brad stretched out on his sleeping bag and made a face. "It beats sleeping on the ground."

"And sleeping on a bed beats sleeping out here too." Nate flung himself onto his sleeping bag. "Haven't we suffered enough already?"

"Come on, Nate; give Gil a break. You've done nothing but gripe since we started this job." Brad rolled over to face Nate. "Why don't you give him a chance?"

"It's okay, Brad. Nate doesn't have to like me. After tomorrow morning, he has to see me only once a week. After six weeks, he won't have to see me again for the rest of his life unless he happens to run into me downtown."

"Which I won't."

"How can you be so sure?" Brad asked.

" 'Cause as soon as I'm old enough to make it on my own, I'm getting out of here. There's got to be a place where people will treat me like I deserve to be treated."

"What we all deserve is . . ."

"I know, I know. We all deserve to be punished for our sins. You don't have to tell me again. I got it the first time." Nate pulled his sleeping bag up to his chin. "I'm going to sleep, so count me out on the sermon for tonight."

Gil lay on his back and stared up at the stars. "Hey Brad, are you asleep?"

"No, why?"

"I was just wondering if you were looking at the stars."

"Yeah, why?"

"I just thought maybe you'd like to learn something about them that my grandfather taught me."

"Okay. I'm not sleepy, that's for sure. There're too many noises out here."

"Those are the crickets and the tree frogs."

"How come they have to be so noisy?"

"I don't know. I guess they're just celebrating the night. Look over there." Gil pointed to the northern sky. "See those four stars that almost form a square? If you look carefully, you'll see what looks like a dipper. You can see three stars that form a curved handle, and those four stars form a bowl. That's called the Big Dipper."

"I've heard of it, but I've never seen it before."

"The two stars on the outside lip of the bowl are called the Pointer Stars because if you draw an imaginary line through those two stars and continue it out about five hand widths, you'll come to the North Star." Gil lay still.

"Okay, I think I see it."

"If you face that star, you are facing exactly north. East will be on your right, west on your left, and south behind you. That's why ship captains and trackers used to use the North Star to find their way at night."

"You mean it's always in the same place?"

"Yes, always. That's why they could depend on it for direction."

"That's kind of like what you've been saying about God, isn't it?"

Gil rose up on his elbow and faced the other boy. "How's that?"

"You said that God never changes. That's just like the North Star; it's always in the same place, and you can depend on it to find your way."

"That's one way to look at it, Brad. God is the One who helps us find our way."

"Do you think He'd help me?"

Before another hour passed, Brad and Gil knelt beside the sleeping bags, and Brad found God's way by receiving Jesus Christ.

The boys had just gotten back into their sleeping bags when they heard a sound. Gil motioned for Brad to be quiet. They lay still and listened.

"I know this is the place, Red. I saw those horses here yesterday afternoon." The voice sounded as if it was right on the other side of the shed.

A deeper voice answered. "Are you sure, Jimbo? I hope you're not wasting my time."

"I'm as sure as I've ever been of anything. I'm telling you this is the place. Look, we'll go inside the shed and I'll show you."

"Not tonight. I want to have a look at these horses in the daylight and make sure you're not feeding me a line. For all I know there could be two donkeys in that shed instead of two show horses. We'll wait 'til tomorrow, then we'll . . ." The voices faded away.

"Did you hear that?" Brad crawled over to Gil. "What do you think we ought to do?"

"Nothing tonight. They didn't know we were here, so they don't know we know. We'll have to come up with a plan tomorrow. Just get back in your sleeping bag and go to sleep."

Gil lay awake for a long time. He went over and over what he and Brad had heard. He did not know what they would do, but he knew Granddad would know. Finally, he fell asleep.

Chapter 19

No one said much as the boys rolled up their sleeping bags and took care of the horses. Nate and Brad would be going home after breakfast. Gil had hoped to have another opportunity to talk to Nate about the Lord, but he seemed even more sullen than usual.

"Did you sleep okay last night, Nate?" Gil poured some sweet feed into the bucket. "You didn't say much after we all turned in."

Nate leaned the pitchfork up in the corner. "Didn't have to. The two of you did enough talking for ten or twenty people."

"I thought you were asleep."

"How could I sleep with all that jabbering going on? Talking about the North Star and how it never changes. And then suckering Brad into believing that God really cares about what happens to us and that someday people will live forever with Him." Nate stood in front of Gil with his arms folded. "It's not true and you know it."

Gil set the bucket down. "It is true and I do know it. I'm just sorry you won't believe it too."

"Oh, don't worry about me. I can take care of myself. I don't need the North Star or anybody to follow to find my way." Nate scooped up his sleeping bag and headed up to the house.

Brad came around the corner. "I heard what he said."

"Do you feel like I suckered you into believing something that's not true?"

"No. In fact, I feel like everything finally makes some sense. I'm with you. I sure wish Nate would believe it too."

Grandma had breakfast on the table when they got to the house. Nate flung himself in one corner of the couch with his hat pulled down over his eyes.

"What's the matter with him?" Granddad wheeled his chair over to Gil.

"He says he's tired of hearing about God and that he can take care of himself." Gil hung his ball cap on his chair. "Brad prayed and asked Jesus to save him last night, and I think it's making Nate a little uncomfortable."

"Well, Brad, that's wonderful." Granddad shook Brad's hand. "You'll have to tell me all about it while we eat. Are you coming, Nate?"

Nate did not even shift his position. "I'm not hungry."

"Suit yourself."

Gil ate in silence. Brad and Granddad didn't seem to notice. He'd have to tell Granddad about the two men later.

Things were pretty quiet after Brad and Nate went home. Gil had not realized how much he had gotten used to having them around. But they'd be back for several Saturdays, and in the meantime he had plenty to worry about besides them.

"It's a shame about Nate." Gil had not heard Grandma come up behind him. He took the basket of laundry from her and carried it to the clothesline. "He could be such a nice kid."

"A nice kid? What makes you say that?"

"I had a chance to talk to him a little bit when he came up to the house, and he was off his guard and not defensive. He was almost sweet."

"Sweet! Nate? I never thought that about him."

"No, he wouldn't have let you see that part of him. He was keeping it well protected. He thinks it's a sign of weakness, I'm sure." Grandma clipped the end of a sheet to the line. "But don't you give up on him. The Lord is working in his heart, and everything you said to him will not be forgotten. You just keep praying for him."

"I will, Grandma. I just don't see how he'll ever change."

"Don't underestimate God's power, Gil. He can change the worst sinner's heart. Just keep praying." Grandma began to hum "Amazing Grace."

Gil stopped by to see Granddad before he went home. He found him before the picture window, his Bible open on his lap.

"Come on in, Gil." He did not turn around. "I was just sitting here thinking about Brad and Nate. And praying for them."

"I've been praying for them too." Gil pulled up a chair. "But there's something else I need to talk to you about."

"What's that, Gil?"

"Last night when we were sleeping out by the shed, Brad and I heard two men talking. They must have come up the lane and didn't see us on the other side of the shed. They were talking about Rattler and Princess."

Granddad turned his chair away from the window. "What about Rattler and Princess?"

"Well, they didn't say much. But from what they said, I think they're planning to steal them."

"What exactly did they say?"

"They didn't say they were going to steal the horses, but one man was telling the other that he was sure that's where they were and that he had seen them the day before. They were going to go into the shed but changed their minds. The one man said he wanted to see the horses in the daylight first."

Granddad rubbed his chin. "It certainly sounds like they were planning something. I'll call Sheriff Keener and tell him what you heard. Then I'll keep a lookout for them from here. You go on home and do whatever you need to do. Tell your dad about it, and the two of you come back here tonight. We'll have to figure out a way to catch them in the act. Just talking about horses isn't a crime, you know." Granddad smiled and ruffled Gil's hair. "Just remember, I'm not the only one looking out for those horses."

"I know, Granddad. I'll see you tonight."

Sheriff Keener, Dad, Granddad, and Gil gathered in Granddad's living room later that evening.

"Well, Walt, did you see anything unusual?" Sheriff Keener balanced his hat on his knee.

"Nothing out of the ordinary. But then I wasn't at the window every second, so they could have come by when I wasn't looking."

The sheriff looked at Gil. "From what you heard last night, do you think they planned to come back tonight?"

"I can't be sure. But it wouldn't surprise me."

"Then I think we'd better be ready for them just in case. Mr. Freeman, maybe you and I can sleep down there where the boys were last night. One of us can keep watch while the other one sleeps. That way if anything happens we'll know about it."

Dad leaned forward. "That sounds like a good plan."

"But Dad, what about me? I'd like to be down there too. After all, one of those horses is mine." Gil rubbed his hands on his jeans. "I can keep watch too."

"We don't know what's going to happen, and it could be dangerous. I'm not sure that would be a good idea." The sheriff shifted his gaze from Gil to Gil's dad.

"I don't know either, Son."

"Please, Dad. I promise I'll be careful."

Gil knew that whatever his dad decided, he would have to abide by. But he couldn't stand the thought of going to bed while Rattler was in danger.

"What do you think?" Dad asked Granddad. "Do you think it's a good idea?"

"I think Gil's responsible enough to be of some help down there. If nothing else, he can run for help if you need it." Granddad laughed. "This sounds almost like a good old-fashioned stakeout."

"I'm afraid it could be serious." Sheriff Keener cleared his throat. "Men like this can be dangerous."

"I know they can, but with your being along, Sheriff, we're not taking too many chances." Gil ran his hands through his hair. "It seems like they're up to something or they wouldn't waste their time coming out to look at the shed in the middle of the night and then come back the next day to see the horses. I don't think these men are really dangerous. They're just looking for a chance to make some easy money."

"All right, Son, you can come along. But we still need to be careful."

Gil spread more straw, making the sleeping place beside the shed a little longer for his dad and the sheriff. He hadn't expected to spend two nights out here. And he sure hadn't expected to be on the trail of horse thieves.

Sheriff Keener came around the corner of the shed. "It looks pretty quiet. We might as well turn in. I'll take the first watch."

The night passed uneventfully. No one came near the shed, and the horses were undisturbed.

"It looks like whoever it was changed his mind," Sheriff Keener said the next morning. "I'll keep my ears open in town and see if anyone's heard anything. But I think we can assume these men are amateurs and got scared off." The sheriff got in his car. "I'll call you if I hear of anything."

The next few days fell into the usual pattern. Nothing out of the ordinary happened, and there was no news from the sheriff. Gil forgot about the two men.

Chapter 20

A few days later, Gil awoke with a start. He heard a knock at his door.

"Gil, Gil, get up!" Dad's voice sounded urgent. "Granddad just called and wants us to come right over."

When they pulled into the driveway at Granddad's, Gil saw the sheriff's car and Julie's family's station wagon. Beyond the house he saw a truck and horse trailer in the pasture. Rattler and Princess were grazing nearby.

"What's going on, Dad?" Gil leaned forward to peer out the front window.

"I guess we'll find out." Dad stopped the car.

Julie met them in the driveway. "Looks like we caught the horse thieves. Actually, Rattler caught them."

"What happened?" Gil tried to see past Julie.

"I think you'd better hear it from Sheriff Keener." Julie led the way across the pasture. Her dad came to meet them.

"They're right over there." Mr. Blakemore pointed to the horse trailer. "Follow me."

Inside the horse trailer two men sat side by side on a bale of hay. Behind them were the saddles, Julie's silver one beside Gil's brown leather ones. Gil looked from Julie to her dad and back at the sheriff. They all seemed to be smiling.

"Is anyone going to tell me what happened?" Gil was getting impatient.

"These are the would-be horse thieves you heard by the shed the other night," Sheriff Keener said.

"Their names are Red and Jimbo, and they came to town with the circus. Jimbo used to be a jockey but joined the circus after he lost his job for trying to steal a horse."

Mr. Blakemore continued. "Red, a horse trainer turned con man, was already with the circus. They joined up and became a team. When the circus leaves town, they go a different direction to sell their stolen goods, usually horses. After they sell the merchandise, they rejoin the circus wherever it is."

"But what are they doing in the trailer?" Gil still didn't understand.

"We were trying to protect ourselves from that killer horse of yours." The bigger of the two men spoke up.

"Killer horse?"

"Yeah, the one with the white mark on his face."

"Rattler? You're kidding. He's no killer."

The smaller of the two men spoke up. "He's a killer all right. He nearly pawed us to death. I think he broke one of my arms and probably broke Red's ankle with those hooves of his."

"He looks pretty calm and peaceful to me." Gil pointed to where Rattler was grazing. "Doesn't look like a killer now."

"Maybe not now. But believe me, he was wild a little while ago." The big man shook his head. "We thought he was coming right into the trailer to finish us off."

"It seems that Red and Jimbo here," Sheriff Keener picked up the story, "decided that last night was a good night to steal one of the horses. Jimbo had seen your horses earlier when you and Julie were up near town the day the elephant got away. He recognized them as show horse quality and told Red about them. Red's the one who wanted to see them in the daylight because he didn't trust Jimbo's judgment.

"They came by the day after you overheard them at the shed, Gil, but they must have come when your grandfather was away from the window. Red spotted Rattler's limp and knew he might not get much money for him, so they decided to take only Princess. But they decided they'd better wait a few days since someone may have seen them near the pasture. That's why they didn't come by the night we were waiting for them.

"To make a long story short, they came last night and coasted down the lane and into the pasture with their lights off. When they got into the shed, they saw the silver saddle and decided to take it, and while they were at it they took the others. Then they went after Princess. She put up a fuss, but they managed to get her out of the shed and almost to the trailer. They hadn't closed the door to the shed, which was their one big mistake. While their backs were turned, Rattler came out the door of the shed after them. He must have known that Princess was in danger. He began to rear and strike at Red and Jimbo, injuring them. They, of course, panicked and jumped in the back of the horse trailer. When your grandfather got to the window this morning, he saw the truck and trailer with Rattler standing guard and Princess grazing nearby. He called me, and you know the rest. After they get treated at the hospital, we'll take them on to jail."

Gil laughed. "Wow, two horse thieves outwitted by a horse." Gil walked over to Rattler. "Rattler, old boy, you've done it again. You came to the rescue of Princess and saved the day. You're terrific. I know you have been a spooker and rambunctious, but you've become a real hero."

A reporter and a photographer for the newspaper came by to get the whole story. That evening a picture of Rattler, Gil, Princess, and Julie was on the front page. Gil's dad had the paper beside Gil's plate when he came in for supper.

"I think this calls for a celebration. What do you think?" Gil's mom poured Gil a tall glass of milk.

"Tomorrow's Saturday, so we've got time to do it." Dad took a swallow of coffee. "How about a cookout at Granddad's? We can invite Julie's family to join us."

"How about Billy's family too?" Gil said. "I told him all about the stakeout, but I'm sure he'd like to know how it ended."

"Sounds good to me. I'll give Grandma a call." Dad got up from the table. Before he could get to the phone, it rang.

"Freeman residence." There was a long silence while Dad just listened. "I think you'd better tell all this to him yourself. Here he is." Dad handed the phone to Gil. "It's for you."

Gil listened carefully, but he could not believe what he was hearing. He tried to give the appropriate responses, but he could hardly make a sound. He did manage to thank the person for calling and said goodbye.

"Well, Son?" Dad was smiling. "What did he say?"

"He said that there's a $10,000 reward out for Jimbo and Red! They're wanted for stealing horses, and the police in two states are looking for them. The owners of one of the horses they stole have been offering this reward for a long time. They said I can get it because it was my horse that cornered them. Can you believe it? $10,000! That's a lot of money!"

Gil swung a leg over his chair and took a big bite of mashed potatoes. He swallowed almost without chewing. "Let's see, after my tithe, I can pay off the rest of my loan from Granddad for Rattler, and I can pay Mr. Snow and Mr. Perkins. Then I'll put the rest in the bank for college." Gil took another bite of potatoes. "Say Dad, you know that college fund for widows' children our church has? I think I'll give my tithe to that, plus a $200 thanksgiving offering. I'll ask that the money go for Billy's college education. He's smart, but he's going to need help with money for college."

"That's a wonderful gesture of friendship, Son. I think the Lord would be pleased." Dad smiled across the table. "But right now, I think you'd better slow down and finish your supper." He laughed. "That money won't do you or anybody else any good if you choke to death on your food."

Gil swallowed another bite. "I'm almost done. Then I'm going to call Granddad about the reward Rattler earned. And tomorrow I'm going to go buy Rattler a bushel of the biggest reddest apples I can find."

APPENDIX A

GRANDDAD'S MOTIVATING BIBLE PRINCIPLES

1. It's too soon to quit.	James 5:11
2. Make up your own mind.	Hebrews 11:25; Joshua 1:7; 24:15; Ephesians 4:23
3. Finish the job.	Acts 20:24
4. A place for everything and everything in its place.	I Corinthians 14:40
5. Honesty is the right policy.	Romans 12:17
6. Keep on the gospel trail.	Proverbs 11:30; II Corinthians 4:3
7. There's a better way.	I Corinthians 12:31; Psalm 18:30
8. Character is belief in action.	James 1:22; Matthew 7:20, 24
9. God made women weaker to be protected and understood.	I Peter 3:7; Ephesians 5:28-29
10. Do right now.	Ecclesiastes 9:10
11. If it is to be, it's up to God working in me.	Philippians 4:13; Ephesians 3:20
12. Giving is love in action.	II Corinthians 9:6-8; I John 3:17
13. Set your goals and plan to reach your goals.	Philippians 3:13; Proverbs 13:12, 19
14. Give thanks in everything, for God is working His will.	I Thessalonians 5:18; Romans 8:28
15. You can do anything God wants you to do.	I Thessalonians 5:24
16. Keep a positive faith attitude.	Hebrews 11:1; Philippians 4:8
17. You were uniquely created to fulfill God's purpose for you.	Psalm 139; Philippians 2:13
18. There is no limit to what you can do if you don't care who gets the credit.	I Corinthians 4:7
19. If the student has not learned, the teacher has not taught.	II Timothy 2:24-26
20. Before you act, get all the facts.	Ephesians 5:17; Proverbs 18:13
21. Love the unlovely.	I John 4:7-8

LIFE-GUIDING TRUTHS ABOUT GOD

God has	By faith we can choose to
Perfect love (Isaiah 40:10-11; I John 4:8-10)	Receive it and share
Infinite wisdom (Isaiah 55:8-9; Romans 11:33-34)	Recognize it and submit
Complete control (Daniel 4:17, 35; Ephesians 1:11)	Trust and rest
Ultimate holiness (Psalm 84:11; I Peter 1:13-16)	Live it and rejoice
Unlimited creativeness (Psalm 19:1-3; Acts 17:24-25)	Enjoy it and praise
Majestic power (Job 37:10-13; Ephesians 3:20)	Claim it and glorify

APPENDIX B
GOD'S WAY TO HEAVEN

Jesus said, "I am the way, the truth, and the life: no man cometh unto the Father, but by me" (John 14:6). "Ye shall die in your sins: for if ye believe not that I am he, ye shall die in your sins" (John 8:24). "Whosoever committeth sin is the servant of sin" (John 8:34). "If the Son therefore shall make you free, ye shall be free indeed" (John 8:36).

"For the wages of sin is death; but the gift of God is eternal life through Jesus Christ our Lord" (Romans 6:23).

"But God commendeth his love toward us, in that, while we were yet sinners, Christ died for us. Much more then, being now justified by his blood, we shall be saved from wrath through him" (Romans 5:8-9).

"For by grace are ye saved through faith; and that not of yourselves: it is the gift of God: Not of works, lest any man should boast" (Ephesians 2:8-9).

Jesus said, "Except a man be born again, he cannot see the kingdom of God" (John 3:3). "For God so loved the world, that he gave his only begotten Son, that whosoever believeth in him should not perish, but have everlasting life" (John 3:16). "For God sent not his Son into the world to condemn the world; but that the world through him might be saved" (John 3:17).

"Repent ye therefore, and be converted, that your sins may be blotted out" (Acts 3:19).

"That if thou shalt confess with thy mouth the Lord Jesus, and shalt believe in thine heart that God hath raised him from the dead, thou shalt be saved. For with the heart man believeth unto righteousness; and with the mouth confession is made unto salvation. For whosoever shall call upon the name of the Lord shall be saved" (Romans 10:9-10, 13).

"But as many as received him, to them gave he power to become the sons of God, even to them that believe on his name" (John 1:12).

"And this is the record, that God hath given to us eternal life, and this life is in his Son. He that hath the Son hath life; and he that hath not the Son of God hath not life. These things have I written unto you that believe on the name of the Son of God; that ye may know that ye have eternal life, and that ye may believe on the name of the Son of God" (I John 5:11-13).

"Therefore being justified by faith, we have peace with God through our Lord Jesus Christ" (Romans 5:1).

"There is therefore now no condemnation to them which are in Christ Jesus, who walk not after the flesh, but after the Spirit" (Romans 8:1).

Jesus said, "Go ye into all the world, and preach the gospel to every creature. He that believeth and is baptized shall be saved; but he that believeth not shall be damned" (Mark 16:15-16).

APPENDIX C
GOD'S COMMANDMENTS

Jesus said,
"Thou shalt love the Lord thy God with all thy heart, and with all thy soul, and with all thy mind" (Matthew 22:37).

1. "Thou shalt have no other gods before me" (Exodus 20:3).
2. "Thou shalt not make unto thee any graven image" (Exodus 20:4).
3. "Thou shalt not take the name of the Lord thy God in vain" (Exodus 20:7).
4. "Remember the sabbath day, to keep it holy" (Exodus 20:8).

Jesus said,
"Thou shalt love thy neighbour as thyself" (Matthew 22:39).

5. "Honour thy father and thy mother: that thy days may be long upon the land" (Exodus 20:12).
6. "Thou shalt not kill" (Exodus 20:13).
7. "Thou shalt not commit adultery" (Exodus 20:14).
8. "Thou shalt not steal" (Exodus 20:15).
9. "Thou shalt not bear false witness against thy neighbour" (Exodus 20:16).
10. "Thou shalt not covet" (Exodus 20:17).

Jesus said,
"If ye love me, keep my commandments" (John 14:15).